A Candlelight Ecstasy Romance®

"WE COULD TRAIN TOGETHER. I BET YOU COULD GIVE ME SOME POINTERS. I MIGHT EVEN COME UP WITH A FEW MYSELF."

When he saw Andy start to tense, Jake tousled her hair. "Then again, maybe you already know it all. You do run like a magnificent gazelle."

Andy blushed. It was his first compliment that didn't have heavy overtones of a standard line.

"You look quite fleet out there on the track yourself," she replied.

"My guess is"—he smiled broadly—"that we could be good for each other. As runners, of course."

"I don't know, Mr. Downing," Andy teased. "First good neighbors, then running partners. What next?"

"Ah, Ms. Howard." He smiled devilishly. "The ball is in your court."

A CANDLELIGHT ECSTASY ROMANCE ®

BUSINESS BEFORE PLEASURE

Alison Tyler

A CANDLELIGHT ECSTASY ROMANCE ®

Published by
Dell Publishing Co., Inc.
1 Dag Hammarskjold Plaza
New York, New York 10017

Dell ® TM 681510, Dell Publishing Co., Inc.

Candlelight Ecstasy Romance®, 1,203,540, is a registered
trademark of Dell Publishing Co., Inc., New York, New
York.

ISBN: 0–440–10857–8

Printed in the United States of America
First printing—April 1984

*To Dad—who always inspired me
with the joy of writing*

To Our Readers:

We have been delighted with your enthusiastic response to Candlelight Ecstasy Romances®, and we thank you for the interest you have shown in this exciting series.

In the upcoming months we will continue to present the distinctive, sensuous love stories you have come to expect only from Ecstasy. We look forward to bringing you many more books from your favorite authors and also the very finest work from new authors of contemporary romantic fiction.

As always, we are striving to present the unique, absorbing love stories that you enjoy most—books that are more than ordinary romance. Your suggestions and comments are always welcome. Please write to us at the address below.

Sincerely,

The Editors
Candlelight Romances
1 Dag Hammarskjold Plaza
New York, New York 10017

CHAPTER ONE

At exactly five minutes to eleven Andrea Howard strode from her garret office on the third floor of the converted town house in the Back Bay section of Boston. Smoothing out some imaginary wrinkles in her soft brown twill skirt, making sure the leather buttons that ran down the front were secure, and checking the lacy tie of her taupe linen blouse, Andy entered Ted Foster's outer office.

Sally Avery smiled up at Andy. "Right on time," she said, glancing at her digital watch. "He's a little behind schedule, but he'll buzz when he's ready for you."

"Thanks Sally." Andy smiled back warmly, lingering at the secretary's desk. "How's Tom coming along?" she asked, a concerned expression puckering her brow. A week ago Sally's husband had been rushed to Mass. General with a mild heart attack.

"Well"—the middle-aged woman grimaced and then grinned—"he's complaining so much at the hospital that they're going to toss him out of there tomorrow. So I guess he's on the road to recovery."

"That's great," Andy said, relieved at the news. Sally and Tom had always been nice to Andy, occasionally inviting her over to their home for dinner. Tom was a master carpenter and he had built a storage unit for Andy shortly before his heart attack.

"You tell Tom for me that it's time he slowed down a little," Andy said, pointing her finger for emphasis.

Sally shrugged. "I'll tell him, but that old fool hasn't listened to a soul for the past fifty-five years." The phone rang, and as Sally swiveled in her chair to reach it, she said quickly, "Thanks again for the lovely flowers. You're a sweetheart."

Andy squeezed the older woman's shoulder affectionately, and while Sally attended to the call, Andy walked over to a nubby beige couch, opened her attaché case, and was immediately absorbed with the final scheduling of next week's research panels. When the buzzer sounded, Andy replaced her mass of papers, and clearing her thoughts, she walked briskly into Ted Foster's office. As she opened the door, she smelled the familiar aroma of old leather mingled with a slightly pungent pipe tobacco that her boss ordered specially from Amsterdam.

"Ah, here she is now," Ted gushed. He was a small, dapper man with graying hair and a pinched expression. It was even more puckered than usual this morning, reminding Andy suddenly of a constipated peacock. The amusing image lifted her spirits.

"Andrea Howard, meet Jake Downing. I've just been telling Jake what an asset you are to this place and how lucky he is to have you here to help him get started."

Their handshake was crisp as they checked each other out. Andy at five feet eight was accustomed to looking most men straight in the eye, but Jake Downing at over six feet forced Andy to tilt her head slightly to face him. As she studied him for the first time, her eyes were drawn to a tiny red scar the shape of a quarter-moon at the corner of his mouth. It gave his smile a slightly cynical appearance. Or was it only the scar? Jake Downing had an aura about him of cool confidence, carrying his tall, lanky body with controlled ease.

Somehow, Andy had imagined a robust, dark man with an overbearing manner. But Jake, fair-haired with a taut, lean body and a healthy tanned complexion, was the exact opposite. He looked as if he would be more at home outdoors than in an office. Only his well-made khaki business suit belied the image. There was a rugged strength about his whole appearance. His craggy, deeply lined face didn't exactly make him look older than his thirty-four years, just fiercer. Compelling dark brown eyes that stared intently at Andy as they nodded a greeting added to her impression of Jake Downing as an exceptionally powerful man.

"It's a pleasure to meet you, Miss Howard." Jake

13

Downing's voice held a questioning inflection as he said the word "Miss."

Purposely choosing not to clarify her marital status, Andy answered, "We're quite informal around here. Everyone goes by first names, Jake."

"Andrea, then." He smiled, flashing even white teeth.

"Andy." She returned his smile, getting a perverse pleasure from correcting him again.

"Ted tells me you head a top-notch research staff." Jake led smoothly into another topic. Andy had to admire him. He didn't fluster easily.

"We manage pretty well, even when we sometimes get a bit overloaded." She addressed the remark to Ted as well, since she'd been on his back for months to let her hire a few more assistants.

"I'm counting on keeping you so busy, Ted here might have to add on a second team." Jake smiled in what Andy viewed as an ingratiating way. Ted didn't think so. He beamed.

"Jake has some great ideas for drumming up new business."

"Really," Andy said dryly. "I'd be interested to hear about them."

Andy knew Jake was observing her closely, and that served to make her even more alert. As Ted droned on in his long-winded fashion about key office policies, Andy tried to stare Jake down. Although Jake intermittently made eye contact with and nods of understanding to Ted, he repeatedly drew his eyes back to hers, that slightly crooked smile dancing on his lips.

14

On the surface Andy continued playing a cool game. But to her surprise her heart was beating far too rapidly. Jake Downing's eyes were more than a little disturbing. In fact everything about him had an unsettling effect on her. She found herself wishing her adversary were short, fat, and balding, instead of so damn virile and attractive.

"Listen, you two"—Ted's direct address forced both of them to focus on him—"it's close to noon, and I've got a luncheon meeting scheduled. Why don't you take off for a bite to eat so you can get to know one another."

It was an order and not a suggestion. Andy gave Jake a look that said, "You don't argue with the boss." Jake appeared delighted with the idea.

"You'll have to pick the spot, Andy," he said in that smooth, resonant voice. "I'm the new guy in town."

Reluctantly she acquiesced. "I guess Charley's would be as good a place as any. I won't be able to spend too much time at lunch. There's a sky-high pile of work waiting for me."

"Never mind the paperwork," Ted interrupted. "This takes precedence. I want Jake to get settled in as soon as possible. I even suggested that you might be able to give him some help in finding a place to live. Can't stay in a hotel for too many days." Ted gave Jake a light rap on the back. "Andy grew up in this town, knows it like the back of her hand. She'll find you a place."

It was only Andy's ironclad will that kept her from literally strangling her boss. Why didn't he simply have Jake move in with her, she fumed. But then Ted Foster more than frowned on personal involvements between staff members, as she so pointedly knew. No, he merely wanted her to make sure his new golden boy was well looked after. Andy hadn't gotten as far as she had without learning not to countermand the boss's orders. But she was damned if she was going to go too far out of her way to make Jake Downing's entry into Horizons Marketing Research, Inc. a bed of roses.

Walking together to the door, their hands both reached the doorknob at the same time, Jake's covering Andy's. Andy felt an unaccustomed fluttering sensation in her stomach at Jake's touch. He stood so close to her she was acutely aware of the musky scent of his after-shave. It was as though an electric shock had bolted through her. In other circumstances she might allow herself to be drawn to the appealing Mr. Downing. After an uncomfortable moment Jake let go.

As they walked down the wide tree-lined boulevard of Commonwealth Avenue, Andy's mind wandered over the past year and a half of her life. She had been less than active socially as she took on more and more responsibility in the company. There was never even a casual get-together with anyone from Horizons. She held to the letter of Ted Foster's mandate about keeping professional and personal lives separate. Since she spent so much of her life at succeeding in her career, she didn't meet many eligible men. Generally Andy found her occasional dates either solely on the make or else tediously boring. Few men sparked her interest.

Suddenly Andy felt Jake's hand on her shoulder, pulling her to a halt and immediately stopping her woolgathering.

"Whoa." He grinned. "I thought I was a fast walker, but you can really put on speed." He glanced admiringly at her long, sculpted legs.

Oblivious to her brisk step, Andy flushed. "I'm used to keeping a fast pace. Sorry." She started to take a step forward, but Jake's strong hand still held her fast.

"Would you be disappointed if we didn't go to Charley's after all?" he asked.

Andy gave him a puzzled look. "No," she said hesitantly. "Not if you don't care to."

"It's too beautiful a day to spend inside a crowded restaurant." He steered her towards Barry's Take-Out Deli a few yards away. "Let's get some sandwiches and go sit in the Public Gardens."

"I thought you were a stranger here." She turned, giving him a suspicious look.

"Even an out-of-towner has heard of the Public Gardens." He chuckled. "Besides, one of my favorite childhood stories was *Make Way for Ducklings.*"

"That's funny, it was one of my favorites too," Andy observed, dropping her archness as she thought about the charming story set in Boston's Public Gardens.

Nearing the deli, it was Andy's turn to bring Jake to a halt.

"If you want to picnic in the gardens, there's only

17

one way to do it." Now she was the one taking charge, steering him back down the street toward the gardens. He followed her lead, casting her a quick grin.

Was her motive that visible, she wondered? Even in casual matters she had no desire for Jake Downing to get the upper hand. This was her turf, and if she had to play companion to this golden boy, she was damn well going to be the one to do the leading.

It was a glorious, sun-dappled Indian summer afternoon, although by all odds early October should have been chillier. Strolling in the fragrant gardens with a compelling man whose dark eyes reflected Andy's appeal would have been idyllic if only the man were not Jake Downing.

Andy guided Jake to an umbrella-covered hot dog stand at the corner of the park.

"Hey, Miss Howard, long time no see." The jovial vendor, whose rotund middle looked like he had consumed more than his share of his own product, beamed at her.

"Good to see you too, Gus. They've been keeping me chained to the office for the past few weeks"—she grinned—"but I can only go so long without one of your gourmet delights. Give me one with the works," Andy ordered, and then before Jake could speak, she added, "Make it two more of the same for my"—she paused for a moment at a loss for how to describe Jake. Then it came to her—"my associate. And two Dr Peppers." She twisted her head toward Jake, who stood slightly behind her. "Okay?"

"Your treat?"

Andy nodded. "Sure, I'll put it on my expense account," she said facetiously. It was worth the treat to watch Jake try to balance two overloaded hot dogs and a frosty can with the motto "Be a Pepper" as they wound their way to the pond.

Sitting on the grass they watched the famous snow-white swan boats lazily cruise the tiny bay of water. Several were docked because the season was nearing a close.

Wiping the edge of his mouth after consuming a quarter of a hot dog in one bite, Jake studied Andy with an amused grin. His stare made her feel self-conscious, but she pretended to be oblivious to him, forcing herself to chew the rubbery-tasting meat. She focused on the ersatz swans.

Out of the corner of her eye she saw Jake's arm move toward her. As his hand neared her cheek, Andy lurched her head sideways, glaring at him indignantly.

"I was only going to wipe off a smudge of mustard on your cheek," he said, laughing. "I don't usually make it a point of attacking my 'associates' in the park."

Furious at his teasing, she grabbed the paper napkin from his hand and brusquely wiped off her cheek. "I'm perfectly capable of managing myself, thanks."

"You also seem perfectly capable of managing other people as well," he said, flicking a blade of grass off his immaculate slacks.

"What's that supposed to mean?" Andy set her barely eaten hot dog on the velvety lawn and faced him.

19

"Do you always decide what and how much your luncheon date will eat?" That cynical smirk that Andy guessed was a frequent expression returned to his face.

"You aren't my date," she blurted, then felt ridiculous for saying it. She'd been heavy-handed in her approach, but it only served to anger her more that Jake was so openly calling her on her behavior. It was also embarrassing.

"Now, my guess is you don't often blush." His cool hand touched her hot cheek briefly.

This time instead of retreating, Andy's own hand flew to her face as if to miraculously erase the flush that Jake had drawn her attention to.

"Look," she said defiantly, "this is a waste of both our time. I really do have an enormous amount of work waiting for me. We can talk later in the day back at my office." On my ground, she reflected, urgently wanting to put some time and distance between herself and this disturbing man.

As she started to get up, Jake's strong hand grabbed her arm, pulling her back to the grass. His fingers slid down to her hand, his light touch enough to hold her still. Andy felt irrationally shaken by the contact, and she fought for composure.

"For two people who are hopefully going to be working together for a long time, we've gotten off to a poor start. Let's have another go at it. Besides, I haven't eaten my second hot dog yet." He regarded the soggy, brown mess with mock longing.

Andy laughed. "Fenway Franks are famous—if you like hot dogs, of course."

20

"Tell me the truth," he said, his voice serious. "Is it something about me personally: my lopsided nose, my overly large feet, the somewhat outdated cut of my suit; or is it simply my less-than-winning charm?"

"I don't follow," she hedged, her eyes darting back to the water.

Jake gently guided her chin so she faced him. "You impress me as a lady who's usually up front. Let's clear the air, okay? We don't have to become lovers or even friends, just simply cordial to each other, with maybe a little honesty thrown in."

His clear, confronting eyes bore into her with such intensity that Andy had a frightening sensation that Jake saw right to her very soul. Her heart began to beat faster. Andy didn't like what was happening to her. The plan had been to hate Jake Downing without complication, willing his lack of success as sales coordinator, ultimately gaining the position she coveted. Her insides were rebelling.

With a breathlessness she hated herself for showing, she said defiantly, "If it's honesty you want, you might as well know that until you appeared on the scene, Ted Foster had as much as promised me your job. And as cocksure as you are that you're going to bring in new accounts by the thousands, I'm not about to stand on the sidelines cheering you on. If you turn out not to be Foster's golden boy after all, I fully intend to take your place."

So, Andy said silently, Ted thought I wasn't aggressive enough, did he? He should hear me now. On second thought, she decided he'd be none too pleased at what he would surely term her mutiny.

The wounds were still raw, the battle with Foster still very much alive. For the past six months Andy had been groomed for the sales coordinator position. Two weeks ago Ted informed her of his decision to hire Downing, an established sales coordinator from Chicago. When she accused Foster of holding a past indiscretion against her, he vociferously denied the charges. She simply had not acquired enough experience. Trying to placate her, he told her Downing would be coming on a six-month trial basis. He wanted Andy to work along with the new man as she had done with his predecessor, Phil Manning. The implication was that if Downing didn't work out, Andy would be that much more prepared to step into the position.

In over eight years of working for Horizons, Andy could recognize a snow job. In her confrontation with Ted, she told him icily that she would stay on for the six months, but only because she was confident an outsider would not be able to step successfully into such a tight-knit organization. At the end of the six months she would either move into the position she deserved, or else she would put on her walking shoes. Being a pragmatist, Andy realized that it would be foolhardy to take any chances. She would have to begin quietly nosing around for another job. There was, unfortunately, always that possibility that the dynamo from Chicago just might work out.

Jake's voice interrupted her thoughts.

"The picture begins to clear," he mused, brushing

back a recalcitrant strand of his sandy hair. "So we're in competition." He studied her classic profile. "Well, I don't know about you, but I thrive on a little healthy competition."

A faint smile crossed Andy's lips as she continued to stare silently ahead of her. She had wanted him to be irate, indignant, to place some distance protectively between them. But he was a lot like her. He didn't back off easily.

"Well, Mr. Downing, you better plan to be on your toes then. I never take defeat lying down." She smirked.

"I'm beginning to wonder whether you take anything lying down," he quipped seductively.

"And, another thing," Andy quickly countered. "Foster has an ironclad rule. No personal involvements among staff. He wouldn't look favorably on your coming on to one of his executives."

"Is that a direct warning?" he asked dryly.

"Let's just call it a piece of helpful advice."

"Well, that's very gracious, considering you've declared open warfare." He grinned, clearly undaunted by her chill manner. "Unless you imagine it might give me some kind of an edge, tell me about yourself. I always like to know about my adversary." Jake's voice held a hint of challenge.

"I'm not sure." She grinned despite herself. "I think I'm safer sticking to name, rank, and serial number."

"You're not my captive—yet." He gave her a mocking look.

"And not likely to be," she said coyly. Stop it,

23

Andrea Howard, she scolded herself. No cavorting with the enemy. But she couldn't deny the tingling feeling she experienced as they bantered flirtatiously back and forth.

Ignoring her own warnings, she said, "You go first. Is Chicago your hometown?"

"Taking charge again." He eyed her with an arched brow. "Okay, I'll play it your way—just to show you what a cooperative guy I am. I'll start at the beginning. Born nearly thirty-five years ago in the town of Madison, Wisconsin. I've got three younger sisters—all of whom idolize their older brother, naturally."

"Naturally," Andy mimicked.

"My father ran a hardware store on Main Street. Dad expected me to take it over one day. Mom had greater expectations. She wanted me to become either a doctor, lawyer, or . . ."

"Indian chief?" Andy interrupted with a grin.

"Sure, if it could bring me wealth and acclaim." Jake laughed.

There was a serious quality behind the banter that drew Andy's attention.

"It was the one thing the folks argued about," Jake said quietly. "I guess in some ways I rebelled against both of them. I never did like anyone governing my choices." He gave her an oddly disconcerting look.

"So you went into sales?" Andy asked quickly, focusing her attention on a wayward blade of grass that had fallen onto her skirt.

"I always was a good salesman." He grinned devilishly. "People always told me I could talk anybody into anything."

"Women especially, no doubt," Andy retorted.

Jake laughed, immediately drawing an unwanted flush to Andy's face. She had so easily fallen for Jake's bait. "I did break the record for magazine subscription sales in high school. At least 90 percent of the subscribers just happened to be women," he teased further.

"And after high school?" Andy asked, refusing to get caught up in his little game. She stared off at the water.

"Off to greater glories," he half whispered.

At Andy's disparaging glint, Jake smiled. "Actually, I won athletic scholarships to the universities of Wisconsin and Chicago. I decided on Chicago. It was farther away from Dad's store. Besides, I liked the idea of life in the Windy City."

"And?" she queried offhandedly.

"Too windy." He grinned.

Jake leaned back on the grass, stretching his long, lanky frame as he crossed his arms behind his head.

"That's the story in a nutshell."

He turned his face from the glaring sun. Andy's eyes openly traced the virile lines of his torso. It didn't surprise her that he had been an athlete.

"What was your sport?" she asked.

"Basketball." He squinted open one eye. "Tiny Archibald was my hero, but not too many six-footers make it to pro ball. Anyway, I don't think I really would have been happy spending my adult life pounding a glorified beach ball on a hardwood floor six months out of a year."

"And are you happy now?" The question was out of her lips before she realized it.

"It's been some time since I viewed life in terms of happiness," he commented more to himself than her, a quizzical expression softening his hardened features. "I've been too occupied getting what I want."

"How about you?" He threw her own question back at her, lifting himself onto his elbows while he waited for her answer.

"You already learned from Ted that I was born and bred in Boston—" she began, pretending he was asking her now to tell him her life story.

"Uh-uh," he taunted. "Play fair."

"You want to know if I'm happy?" She busied herself tucking a straw-colored strand back behind the tortoiseshell clasp that kept her shoulder-length hair in place. "I already admitted to you that I'm not. Remember. You're in the job that I want." She curved her lips in a cool smile.

"Is all your happiness based on your rise to fame and fortune at Horizons?" Impetuously he snatched the comb that she'd just busied herself adjusting. Her shining hair came cascading around her face. Andy quickly grabbed the fastener from his hand, deftly putting it back in its proper place.

"I'm afraid we're going to have to postpone my treatise on happiness for another time. I have a staff meeting in less than ten minutes." She was on her feet and at the trash container before Jake stood.

Catching up to her, he said, "Don't forget about my housing problem. Why don't I meet you after work and we can go over some ideas?"

"I have plans for dinner." Andy hurried down the path, but this time Jake had no difficulty keeping up with her.

"I can pick your brain over a cocktail, then. Can't stay in a hotel forever." He imitated Ted Foster expertly.

"Contrary to Ted's belief, I don't moonlight as a real estate agent."

It was that crooked smile of his that did her in. The little scar all but winked at her. She relented. "Well, maybe a quick drink, and I can at least give you some idea about the neighborhoods nearby."

"Good. Then it's a date." He winked. Suddenly he wet his index finger with his tongue and traced a line down Andy's cheek. The movement was so unexpected and surprisingly sensuous that Andy froze, her mouth falling open.

"Just some remnants of mustard." He grinned seductively. "Wouldn't want you returning to work with any telltale signs."

Without a word Andy started walking fast and furiously down the path. But this time Jake's step proved even brisker, forcing Andy to have to hurry to keep pace with him.

CHAPTER TWO

Sunday morning, as dawn was just breaking through
the clouds and a steady drizzle wet the pavement,
Andy found herself almost alone on the running path
around the UMASS soccer field. She had already
clocked over five miles, but her body felt so well
tuned this morning that she decided to keep going.
The driving aches and pains that assail all runners
had finally subsided, leaving a tingling numbness
that allowed Andy to proceed with renewed ease.

It had been the first time all week that her running
was on target. She hadn't skipped a single day, but
she continually found her breathing off, her usually
steady rhythm out of kilter, and the cramping sensations in her body more intolerable. Today finally
everything was back to normal. As she continued to
pace herself, her mind floated back to the past week.

After their Monday afternoon drink, Andy had

only seen Jake briefly while he was on his way to a meeting with his salesmen. He had nodded casually to her as they passed in the hall. Officially he would begin work tomorrow, but she knew he had been in and out of the office quite a bit.

Horizons was abuzz with his arrival. People continually offered opinions and made guesses as to his background and his personality. Andy could have told them a thing or two, but she kept silent. Her staff, knowing that she had put in for Jake's job, were not surprised by her indifferent manner. What irked her the most were the comments she frequently heard in passing from some of the female staff about Jake's sex appeal.

Who was she kidding, she thought as she completed another lap, the rain keeping up its steady drizzle. Hadn't his rugged virility struck her at their first meeting? Jake was one of those men whose rough features and imperfections only added to his masculine attraction. And in large part that attraction had been the cause of her feeling so out of sorts and distracted all week long. She kept finding him popping up in her mind. It was bad enough when it happened at work, but when he appeared uninvited in her dreams, it was insufferable. And no matter how much she tried to will him from her thoughts, he kept right on resurfacing.

Andy brought herself back to the day at hand. Now the rain was pelting down. She was amazed that she had run another mile. Her thoughts about Jake had absorbed her so thoroughly that the added mile had clipped by unnoticed. Andy became aware of her soaked tee shirt emblazoned with the words I Love Boston and her equally drenched powder-blue shorts. Her lightweight New Balance running shoes squished with each pace. Running in this kind of rain was crazy. She could easily slip on the soggy turf and injure herself seriously. Better to finish the lap and call it a day.

Another crazy runner was still out on the track. He was a good hundred yards in front of her. Andy had been half-aware of him the whole time, unconsciously setting her pace to his long steady stride. She regarded him admiringly as he ran. He was a true runner, but then who else would have ventured out on a day fit only for ducks. Andy watched the way his body moved with elegant ease and grace, the taut firm muscles of his arms and legs working in perfect harmony. He was beautiful to observe. His drenched white tee shirt revealed a strong, broad back while his brief white running shorts accentuated the slim hips and long powerful legs. Watching him off in the distance, Andy felt her breathing start to race erratically, and she flushed with the realization of where her reveries about the phantom runner were leading her. It was definitely time to stop running. Ironically, the rain was finally letting up.

As she came to a halt, the other runner was going through his cool-down exercises. He bent forward, stretching the muscles in his leg. Andy stood watching, once again fascinated by his physique. When he turned around to face her, Andy let out a mortified gasp.

"What the hell are you doing here?" She stood rooted to the spot, unable to believe her eyes.

"What does it look like I'm doing?" Jake immediately began some more stretches, ignoring her gaping stare. After a few moments he paused again, regarding her with a disapproving glance. "You should know better than to stand around after that workout," he chided.

Andy knew he was right, and she was bound to pay the price later with horribly aching, sore limbs. Warm-up and cool-down stretching exercises were as important as the running itself. But right now she was transfixed, unable to move.

Looking down at her legs, Jake grinned. "I was pretty sure those gorgeous gams of yours had some other function than to merely drive me wild with lust."

"Do you have to be so crude?" she sneered scornfully.

"I guess you just bring out my basest emotions," he said, baiting her. "And you are not making things better now." His eyes traveled from her glowing face down to her clinging tee shirt. Andy followed his gaze, realizing as she did that the rain had made the thin cotton transparent and the rounded curves of her breasts were provocatively displayed, the nipples tautly protruding.

Ignoring her discomfort, he tossed his wet towel around his neck saying, "It's a good thing I happened to be here today. Some masher might have been lurking in the bushes, and if he feasted his eyes on you, he would have eaten you for breakfast."

31

"I think I would have rather taken my chances with the masher," she retorted, arms akimbo.

Andy threw him one last fiery glance and pivoted around. A strong, hard hand clasped her shoulder as she turned her back to him.

"Your muscles are as tight as steel," he said, pressing in against the hardness. Andy took a step forward as his other hand slipped up to her neck. Slowly, rhythmically, he massaged the tense muscles. His grasp held Andy still, but she suddenly didn't want to move. Jake's fingers maneuvered her shoulders with expert proficiency, releasing the tightness. Andy was held mesmerized by the motion and the exquisite sensations his manipulations created. As his hands traveled down to the base of her spine, his knuckles pressing deeply into the muscles in her back, Andy's body bent forward of its own volition, to allow a more penetrating massage. A moan of satisfaction escaped her lips as his fingers returned to her shoulders.

Now his hands again massaged her neck, his fingers entangling themselves in the loose wisps of hair that had escaped the ponytail she always wore when she ran. In a flash, the barrette was opened, sending her hair tumbling down around Jake's hands. His magical fingers began to knead her scalp. Andy had never felt anything so wonderfully relaxing. Her whole being gave in to the hypnotic spell Jake was weaving.

When in a low, husky voice he commanded her to turn around, in a trance Andy pivoted back to face him. His eyes sparked with gleaming intensity. Andy found herself drawn again to that tiny scar that twitched slightly now as his eyes bore into her. Jake's fingers languidly traced the lines of Andy's face, gliding over her firm jawbone, the accentuated cheekbones, and then delicately following the faint lines about her eyes. He lingered at the sensitive points below her earlobes, again pressing lightly with a circular motion. Andy's lips parted in delight, and she tilted her head back to savor the caress. Her body was vibrantly alive, tingling with pleasure.

This time when Jake's large, powerful hands found her shoulders again, he pressed into the muscles for only a second before he pulled Andy toward him. She offered no resistance, her body feeling completely weightless. Only fleetingly did she wonder what had become of all her firm resolve. Feeling almost disconnected, she watched his mouth descend as she lifted her head to meet his lips. Their rain-drenched garments offered no barrier to the intimate sensation of their bodies pressed tightly together, generating a mutual heat that denied the chill in the air. The blend of aromas: sweet wet grass, Jake's musky after-shave, and the heady pungency of their damp bodies' own scents, was intoxicating. She clasped her hands tightly around his neck, allowing his kiss to deepen. A dizzying rush of feeling swept over Andy as the power of his hard, taut body engulfed her.

At that very moment two teenage girls came jogging by, slowing to gaze with open curiosity as the couple embraced. Poking each other in that half-embarrassed, half-fascinated way, they started to giggle. The sound of their laughter brought Andy back to her senses. With sudden force she pushed Jake away from her. He looked somberly into her large, horrified eyes.

Andy couldn't meet his penetrating gaze. Her mind was reeling. How could she have lost control like that? Stunned at how easily she had succumbed to Jake's seduction, she had an intense desire to bolt. There was nothing stopping her. Jake was silent, his hands at his sides. But she knew she wouldn't run.

Forcing her eyes to return his look, she said, "I know I asked for that, but never again." The hardness in her tone was coupled with a breathlessness that still remained from their embrace, her voice sounding deep and throaty.

"That's too bad." He answered with forced jauntiness. "I enjoyed it thoroughly."

"Jake, I am adamant about keeping my personal and professional lives separate." Her words sounded ridiculous after what had just occurred between them, but now that this reason had thankfully returned, Andy once again had her guard firmly in place.

"For someone who shows such delicious abandon, it's too bad your principles are so juvenile." He regarded her with cool disapproval.

"I call it smart business sense," she declared. "And what about you? Just another guy out on the make. Sure, you're in a new town, new on the job, lonely even. Might as well seduce an attractive colleague for some fast action."

"You really do surprise me. I figured you for a

strong, self-confident woman. But the truth is you're one insecure lady."

"What is that supposed to mean," she challenged, but there was a growing feeling of discomfort inside her as Jake began to hit on some sensitive spots.

"Does every man who shows an interest simply want to throw you in the sack and then abandon you?" Some of the harshness had gone out of his tone.

"That's ridiculous. I don't feel that way at all." A cold, clammy sensation forcibly attacked her as she stood rigidly still.

"You're a tough cookie, on the outside, but I bet that underneath your cool veneer is one scared young woman. You've thrown yourself into your work, convinced that getting ahead would somehow protect you from the hard, cruel world. It's still hard and cruel." He paused for a moment, studying her. Then in a soft tone he added, "I'm not your enemy. I'm simply a guy who got hired for a job that you wished you had been offered. That's my crime." He paused once more, and then those piercing brown eyes gazed at her in intimate knowledge. "Or maybe there's something else—something that keeps that enticingly sexy side of you at bay. Something that scares the living daylights out of you."

Jake's words had a forceful effect. A tear escaped her eye, rolling traitorously down her cheek. "What makes you think you know me so well?" she uttered in barely a whisper.

"Maybe because in many ways we're a lot alike.

We're both fighters, and we're both runners. And not just on the track." He gazed at her knowingly.

"I dislike hearing I'm immature, frightened, and running away from myself." She studied him with alacrity. "I do have some finer qualities, you know?" A faint smile played across her lips.

"I know," he teased.

"Jake, this is serious. I may be attracted to you, but there is no way I'm going to get caught up in any tacky after-hours fun and games again."

"Again?" He regarded her with curious interest.

The word had slipped out. She knew he'd hear about her relationship with Ken Haggerty soon enough, and she knew it would be the version everyone believed was true. Right now she hadn't the strength to go into it.

With a finality that belied her churning insides, she said, "Let's keep our distance. I know we have to work together for the time being. There's no getting around the fact that your sales team interfaces with my research crew. And Foster has made it plain that I'm to be helpful. And I will. At work. Beyond that, stay away."

Andy didn't wait for a response. And this time when she turned to leave, no hand reached out to grab her. Jake didn't say a word, and Andy had no idea what he was thinking. As she started down the path, she willed her mind blank.

It was several minutes before she sensed she was being followed. The streets were particularly deserted this morning, what with it being Sunday and a dismally dreary day at that. Walking alone around

Boston's streets never disturbed her, even though she had heard enough about muggings and worse. No one had ever bothered her. Now the growing sense that each corner she turned someone else turned after her began to put Andy on edge. Coming to another corner, she turned abruptly to confront her pursuer.

It was Jake, leisurely strolling up the street. She couldn't believe that after all she had said to him just minutes ago he would have the audacity to follow her home. She waited, her arms crossed defiantly in front of her as he approached. A nonchalant, casual smile played upon his lips as he met up with her.

"Are you totally dense"—she attacked—"or simply insensitive?"

"Neither, I hope," he answered smugly.

"Then why are you following me?"

"I am not following you."

"Have it your way," she said, exasperated. "If you want to make an ass of yourself, be my guest."

Andy blasted down the block. She couldn't hear Jake's footsteps, but she knew instinctively that he was still behind her, maintaining a slight distance. Turning one last corner, her home came into view.

Andy's house was in the middle of a street adorned with wispy-looking, newly planted trees encircled by tiny wire fencing. Several of the brownstones, including Andy's, had been renovated. A few others were actively in the process of being redone or were boarded up waiting to be sold. Still some remained in their old, beaten-up condition. As Andy passed one of these, some local kids sitting on the stoop called out a greeting. Andy waved back but didn't stop to chat with them as she often did. She knew Jake was still behind her, and she was preparing herself for a final confrontation when she got to her front door.

As she now expected, Jake caught up with her as she retrieved her key from the back pocket of her shorts and opened the door. She had purposely paused there, waiting to face him.

"Now what?" she challenged.

"Now we step inside." He pushed the door open wider and entered the long, dark lobby, stopping by a row of brass mailboxes.

"Jake, I don't know what you think you're going to gain by following me home like this. I've said everything there is to say back at the track."

"And I told you I was not following you," he repeated with innocent eyes.

"Then what are you doing here?" She was incensed.

"I live here." He traced his finger across the mailboxes, stopping at 1B. Andy's eyes followed the movement. It was true. Jake's name, newly printed, was Scotch-taped on the box.

"But that's the apartment I told Nancy Dawber about three weeks ago. She was planning to sublet it," Andy blurted.

"I guess you haven't been over to Accounting this past week."

Andy shook her head dumbly.

"Nancy had a sign up on the bulletin board asking if anyone wanted to take over a sublet. Turned out she couldn't get out of her old lease and was stuck with two places. I jumped at the chance."

"But you can't live here," she sputtered.

"I do." He laughed. "You were the one, after all, that sold me on this area. Remember?"

She had included, rather reluctantly, a description of the South End along with the other neighborhoods when they had gotten together over drinks last Monday, but it had seemed farfetched to imagine he would end up here, of all places.

"Don't play games with me, Jake. You knew damn well I didn't want you anywhere around here, and certainly not right under me."

"An interesting choice of words. Freud would have quite a go at that." He chuckled.

Jake's laughter was the final straw. "There may be nothing I can do about your living here, but you had better get one thing straight. I don't want to see you, hear you—I don't want to even know you once we leave that office. So get any ideas about me out of your head."

"Listen to me now," he said dryly. "You may be attractive, but you are not God's gift to mankind. If you think I'm going to spend my time plotting ways to seduce you, forget it. You've made it perfectly clear where you stand." With a flourish he tapped the rounded curve of her shoulder. "And frankly, Scarlett, I don't give a damn." Gable incarnate, he swaggered down the hall.

CHAPTER THREE

Andy flew upstairs to the refuge of her own apartment. As she slammed the door shut, her first thought was that if Jake Downing wouldn't move, then she would. She even extracted the Real Estate section from the *Sunday Globe* and spread it open on her living-room floor.

As soon as she spied the Apartment listings, she knew what she was doing was ridiculous. She closed the paper with finality and sat up cross-legged on the plush chestnut rug. She examined her modest but well-proportioned living room with new awareness. Andy loved this place. Maybe it was only two rooms divided by a galley kitchen so narrow that if Dolly Parton squeezed in, she'd never make it out again. Ample compensations for its size were the working fireplace set off by an opulently carved silvery-white marble mantel and the tall bay-windowed alcove, both of which were remnants of past glory.

No man was going to make her give up her home. Jake, in his inimitable fashion, had made it clear he would keep his distance, and Andy decided she would simply ignore him. After all, she reminded herself, Mrs. Tobias in 1C might be a phantom for all Andy saw of her. On the other hand, she mused ruefully, Jake might be a fiendish poltergeist.

Andy's stomach grumbled. She hadn't eaten yet. Everything was out of whack this morning. She was so rattled that she hadn't even stripped off her soaking-wet running clothes. Grabbing a slice of health bread from the refrigerator, Andy spread some apple butter on it. Munching it with determination, she walked into her bedroom. After consuming enough bites to ease her hunger pangs, she rested the half-eaten slice on her white bureau and got undressed.

The vibrating jets of the steaming hot shower pulsated down on her neck and shoulders. The stimulation always eased the tightness in her body, especially after a run. This morning as Andy closed her eyes to give herself up to the massage, her mind immediately flew back to Jake. Jake with his magic fingers, unknotting her tense muscles and undoing her determined principles. She had kissed him with delicious abandon. Suddenly all her defenses had vanished, and she had given herself up to him with a passion that had been locked away. Even when she had been involved with Ken Haggerty, she had always held back a little.

So why had she let herself, for that brief moment,

open up so fully to Jake? Typically, a slew of rationalizations surfaced. But this time Andy did not buy them. She faced the truth. There was something about Jake that drew her to him on an incredibly primal level. Even that first meeting, when their hands had accidentally touched, Andy sensed an electricity, the sparks warning her to be on guard.

She tried to fathom the secret of his vitality. He wasn't handsome in the traditional sense. His confrontational style made her acutely uncomfortable. And Andy had never responded favorably to the teasing, seductive maneuverings at which Jake seemed so adept. If, as he had so dramatically told her, she was not God's gift to mankind, he was certainly no great prize to womankind, even if his impersonations were uncanny.

Rubbing herself down briskly with a plush terry towel, Andy stepped out of the bathroom. Once dry, she drew her hair up into the towel, skillfully knotting it into a turban. Studying herself in her full-length mirror, naked save for her makeshift headdress, Andy smiled. She could have been Queen Nefertiti having just stepped out of her scented milk bath awaiting the arrival of her lover.

Again Jake's compelling image reappeared. A shiver ran down her spine as she let herself imagine Jake standing there, those dark, all-seeing eyes intently gazing on her slender body. Did he find her breasts too small, her legs, from years of running, too muscular, her hips not shapely enough? Then she felt those large, powerful hands back on her hips, his fingers encompassing the narrow expanse, drawing her to him, so that she could experience the force of his own desire.

Andy's mind stripped Jake of his white tee shirt and shorts. Instantaneously they were lying together on the cool green grass, her lover's hard, hot, deeply tanned body pressed on top of her. His long muscular limbs entwined around her, the golden downy hairs of his broad chest infusing her swelling breasts with a voluptuous tingle.

Together they were transported through time and space. Against the backdrop of majestic stone pyramids, and the clear cool waters of the Nile, the tall, golden-haired lover, his magnificent body glistening under the steaming Egyptian sun, beheld his exquisite queen. He was her slave, who had stolen her off to his hideaway. He was consumed with passionate longing—his turn at last to be her master. Enraptured fingers cherishingly traced her voluptuous curves, firing her body with desire. Slowly his mouth followed the trail his hands had blazed, his sensuous lips burning her neck, then her hibiscus-scented shoulders with each kiss. Inexorably his wanton mouth sought her erect rosy nipples, devouring each in turn. His hard lips lingered for a moment in the velvety soft valley between her breasts before their slow, sensual descent down her silken body.

Her fervent gasp for breath as the fantasy intensified was so audible it wrenched Andy back to the present. When she peered into the mirror now, her nipples were hard with desire, and tiny beads of perspiration shone on her forehead. She felt oddly embarrassed. The fantasy itself wasn't disconcerting, but the fact that the lover had been Jake, the man she had so self-righteously scorned, knocked her for a loop.

Maybe Jake Downing really was a demon. With sudden clarity Andy was certain that she was not going to be able to exorcise him. Those gleaming devilish eyes had completely captured her.

And Andy had spurned him. For all her newly acknowledged feelings, her head told her she had been right. Again she remembered with harsh clarity the pain and humiliation that had been the end result of her whirlwind affair with Ken. When she had first become a research coordinator, Ken was her department head. She had gotten to know him casually while she was still a research assistant, and knew that he had been instrumental in getting her the promotion. When he first began asking her out, it was on the pretext of some after-hours business. Initially Andy accepted his invitations because she felt so grateful to him for his help.

Ken Haggerty had charm gushing out of every pore, and Andy was a complete sucker for his attack. By the time summer started, she was convinced she was falling in love with him and equally certain his feelings were the same. Ken told her he was legally separated from his wife, emphatic about the fact that divorce proceedings were already under way. Of course the divorce never materialized, and when Andy confronted him with his deceit, he had the nerve to suggest that she might enjoy the mistress role even more than that of a wife. After all, he declared smugly, men were always more romantic with their lovers than their spouses.

The worst part of the whole sordid affair was that everyone at work was convinced Andy was sleeping with Ken solely for the purpose of advancing her career. And Ted was irate that Andy had so cavalierly disregarded his mandate about personal involvements at work. "Especially," he had told her sneeringly, "with married staff." Ken's subsequent transfer to another company and Andy's staunch determination to reassert her integrity finally quelled the sly innuendos, the not-so-subtle propositions from other eager execs, and Ted's disgruntlement.

If her relationship with Ken had been a disaster, then involvement with Jake spelled devastation. Fantasy aside, Jake was taboo. With renewed anger, she saw only too clearly the wily ways of her arch rival. He was ready to take Horizons by storm, only there was one annoying hitch. A woman in the company with some clout who planned on giving him a hard time. What better way to get her off his back than to ply her with seduction. Besides, she was certain Ted would not overlook a second entanglement. This one could lose her any further promotions. Maybe Downing was on to that too. Surely Ted had already given Jake his "no sleeping where you work" spiel. Given Foster's chauvinistic style, she knew Jake would not suffer the same fate as she would.

"Oh, good, you haven't submerged yourself in piles of paperwork yet. I need to have you check out

45

some of the data from the phone survey on Robinson's Quick-Set."

Larry Butson, one of Andy's newest and most energetic research assistants, crossed the small office in three brisk strides, easing his large frame into the brown and white director's chair across from Andy's desk. He was a bulky, robust man in his mid-twenties with a shock of carrot-red hair, a neatly trimmed goatee, equally red, and a winning smile.

His smile this morning was short-lived as he met Andy's less-than-warm eyes.

"Oops, not in a good mood this morning, I see. Tough weekend?" he queried lightly.

Andy was fond of Larry. When he had first started working for her a few months ago, he had made a couple of innocent passes. Andy set him straight from the beginning, and since then they had developed not only a comfortable working relationship, but they had become friends as well. His good-humored flirtatiousness was especially harmless now that he had a new girl friend.

Andy smiled back at him. "You should know by now that I'm never terribly cheerful first thing Monday morning when I have to face all of this." She gestured, grimacing, at her desk top. What she didn't add was that she'd also had a lousy night's sleep. After finally falling off around two in the morning, she woke up well before dawn. Unable to get back to sleep, she slipped into her running clothes and went down to the track. She was well into her routine by the time the sun came up. Andy refused to admit to herself that she had gone running so early to avoid the possibility of meeting Jake on the track again.

Stifling a yawn, Andy took the report from Larry. Studying the last two sheets, she frowned. "Who worked up the correlations on the last set of questions?"

"Sandra." He grinned, well aware of Andy's frequent dissatisfaction with his co-worker's performance.

"That woman is going to drive me up a wall," Andy groaned. "Why didn't she do a Q Sort?"

"You know Sandra?" Larry sighed. "She always tries to take a couple of shortcuts."

"Well, there's no way we can present a report to Robinson without figures on color preference based on age as well as socioeconomic status."

"I didn't think you would let it through this way," Larry said as she handed him back the report.

"Do me a favor, Larry." Andy gave him a beseeching smile. "Run the stats yourself. I know you're working on the Soloman ski account, but I'm not up to a hassle with Sandra this morning." One day this week she would have to lay down the law with her inept assistant. If she didn't shape up, Sandra's days were numbered.

Larry gave her a mock salute. "At your service, boss. Especially if it will put those sparkling emeralds back into your gorgeous eyes."

"It will help, believe me." Andy grinned. "Hey, Larry," she added as he started towards the door, "you're a real pal."

"Always the friend, never the lover." He sighed with feigned despair, blowing her a kiss as he exited.

After Larry returned to his computer, Andy roughed out the protocol for Colonel Winston's Breakfast Grits survey. She had a feeling that the colonel was going to be disappointed to learn that "Beantown" was not ready to become "Grittown." Nonetheless, she was determined to design a top-notch multilevel evaluation. Who knows—she chuckled out loud—that entrepreneurial genius may be on to something at that.

"Care to share the joke?"

Andy looked up to see Jake leaning against the doorjamb, hands in his pockets. Something in his posture suggested that he had been standing there watching her for a while.

"Did you want to see me about something?" she asked sharply, effectively masking the somersault her stomach had just completed.

With a wry smile he sauntered into the office, closing the door behind him. He perched himself on the edge of her desk.

"Now, is that any way to welcome a new employee to the fold?" he mocked.

"I thought I had done that already," Andy answered coolly, and then realizing how Jake would interpret her statement, quickly added, "Last week, in Ted's office."

The tack-on was too late. Jake grinned. "You're right. How could I have forgotten?"

Andy groaned. "I should have known better than to think you would stop playing your little games."

48

"Come on, Andy, lighten up. I'm only teasing you so that you'll stop acting so pompously professional." He narrowed his eyes, and edging toward her, he scanned her body. "You've even dressed the part."

"And what's wrong with what I'm wearing?" Andy snapped, looking down at her man-tailored navy suit, her pin-striped shirt accented with a modified bow tie. She'd coveted it for weeks in the window of Ann Taylor's, and when it had gone on sale, she snatched it up. Even so, the price made her a little green.

Flicking the bow tie with his index finger, he merely shook his head. "I prefer you in tee shirt and shorts."

"I'm sure you would," she said coolly, determined not to rise to the bait.

"I missed seeing you running today," he said pleasantly.

"I make it a point of running solo," she countered.

"Just testing you." He grinned. "But I see the ice hasn't thawed. You know you're really making a big mistake. I make a great neighbor. I never play my African tribal music after three A.M. or have disco parties more than twice a week. My Great Dane only howls before meals, and best of all, I snore only when I sleep."

Jake won. Andy broke down and started to laugh. "Well, I better warn you that I'm an awful neighbor," she said between giggles. "My alarm clock radio blasts the entire building awake at five A.M. every morning. That includes weekends. My pet cobra loves to wander. And what's more, I run in place twenty minutes each evening—with my wooden clogs on."

"So that's why the plaster on my ceiling looks as though it had seen a few earthquakes," he responded gravely.

"And that's not the worst of it," she murmured, quickly casing the room. "If this gets out, I'm done for."

"Mum's the word," Jake swore, raising his right hand in earnest promise.

"Well," she whispered conspiratorially, "by day I'm your average middle-class working girl, but every night I bring in a truckload of illegal aliens and we make bootleg wine." She looked at Jake with narrowed eyes. "Have you ever heard two dozen sets of feet stomping grapes?"

"Now, that sounds serious," he said, biting down on his lip as he rubbed his chin contemplatively. "But you know the old saying, 'If you can't lick 'em, join 'em.' "

They both burst into laughter. Finally when they sobered up, Jake regarded Andy seriously. "How about it? I've never made an enemy of a neighbor before I even moved in all my furniture." He eyed her with a questioning brow. "Truce?"

"Truce," she said, relenting. "But I'm only agreeing to reserve judgment about you as a neighbor. As for the rest, what I said before still holds."

"Fair enough. At least when I come begging a cup of sugar, I'll know you won't slam the door in my face." Jake eased off the desk, and with a formality that Andy knew was an imitation of her own last week, he extended his hand.

A completely crazy impulse overcame her. With a sweeping gesture she reached for his hand, brought it to her lips, and lightly kissed his palm. She wished she had a camera to capture Jake's astonished expression. With an impish grin, Andy said, "Welcome to Horizons, Mr. Downing."

"Now that's a welcome I won't forget."

The truce lasted until Thursday afternoon. Actually, looking back, Andy decided it began to falter as early as Wednesday morning. That day Ted asked Jake to share with the staff some of his experiences at the marketing firm he had worked with in Chicago. Not only did Jake describe his previous company as extremely efficient, creative, and productive, he went on to give a critical analysis of his current place of employment. No one, including Andy, got off the hook. Jake managed to say something negative or, at the very least, moderately derogatory about everything from the way the secretaries handled the mail to the way lines of communication failed between middle and upper management. Where the research staff was concerned, Jake claimed they lacked a sense of flair in their reports to clients.

Lecturing now, Jake announced, "Businessmen do not respond well to tedious, academic papers and incomprehensible statistical jargon. Give them the same information with pizzazz—video animation, slide presentations, computer graphics . . ."

"Very snappy, Jake," Andy interrupted. "Maybe

we could hire belly dancers, print our data on their stomachs, and let them dance the info for our clients," she said with a sarcastic bite.

"Now you're cooking," he tossed back, dark eyes glittering. "That's one I'd missed."

"Maybe you could save it for your sales approach," Andy retaliated, the tiny pulse in her throat starting to beat faster.

"Too tame, much too tame." He grinned, winking.

Andy was too annoyed even to listen to Jake's zealous delineation of his endlessly creative sales campaign.

Wednesday afternoon she spent a good hour trying to calm down her irate staff, who claimed they weren't about to kowtow to Jake Downing's bizarre requirements for presentations. Luckily, Andy had always had a solid working relationship with her staff. They not only respected her as their boss, they liked her as a person. She might be demanding, but she was basically caring, supportive, and there in a pinch. When Andy assured them that Jake's job was only to bring in the business and that she'd decide how the report went out, they rallied to her side.

"Anyway," she summed up complacently, "if Jake really practices what he preaches, we may not have to cope with him here for long." The fantasy of his imminent downfall finally appeased everyone, most of all Andy.

Let him try some of his creative ideas on the staid Boston business community, she thought smugly. I'll be in his job sooner than I imagined.

Thursday morning was the first day Andy was to

go out with Jake on some of his calls. That morning Andy had walked to work alone. She'd heard Jake leave his apartment, but his footsteps never sounded on the stairs. When Andy heard the outer door shut, she uttered a mild expletive and timed exactly ten minutes on her watch before starting off to work. If Jake didn't want to walk with her, that was just fine. And if he was playing a little game, testing to see if she was going to make a first move and go knocking on his door, then he was going to wait till hell froze over.

Andy suddenly laughed to herself, remembering her childhood days when she and her friends spent hours on end doing "wait till" jokes—wait till the cookie crumbles; wait till Niagara Falls; wait till hell freezes over. Why was it Jake so often brought out the adolescent in her? For years now she had carefully honed a sleek, sophisticated style when it came to dealing with men. And she had handled with total aplomb some of the slickest hotshots. Jake had come along, and she had started blushing and fighting, plus devoting more time than she cared to admit to fantasies of upping him at every turn. And unfortunately, those weren't the only fantasies she found herself having. She was going to have to get hold of herself or Jake was going to win this one after all. There, she scolded herself, you're doing it again. Still keeping score!

Jake was tied up in meetings for the morning, so they didn't get on the road as early as they had planned. Then the company car that was assigned to Jake had some problem with the radiator, so they had to go through the typical bureaucratic red tape to get another car out of the car pool. It was after eleven by the time they hit Route 128.

"I took a few notes with me this morning," Andy said, all business as they cruised along. "I've been up to Hillcrest and to Franklin Brothers several times." She pulled out her black leather notebook and began giving Jake a rundown on the types of product studies she had done for both companies. She followed with a thumbnail sketch of the men with whom she and Jake would be meeting.

Jake listened without interruption. Finally, when she'd finished, he observed, "You seem tense. Is it my driving?"

They both knew perfectly well it wasn't his driving. He maneuvered the green sedan with expert ease, maintaining a leisurely speed.

"Have you listened to anything I told you?" Andy questioned indignantly, vowing not to let the conversation take any turns she didn't want it to.

"Every word." Jake smiled. "You obviously know quite a bit about this end of the business."

"I should," Andy snapped. "I went out with Phil Manning often enough."

She thought ruefully of the contrast between her comfortable, relaxed outings with Phil and the tension and unease she felt sitting next to Jake. Phil, old enough to be her father, had taken a warm, paternal interest in Andy. She, in turn, was fond of him and valued his supportive instruction. She most definitely had no desire to be further educated by Jake.

"So you're still uptight about the job." Jake's voice

held a hint of sympathy, but Andy wasn't convinced it was completely sincere.

"I guess this is rubbing your nose in it," he added. "Having to take me around."

"It's all part of the drill," Andy said cuttingly. "Hey," she yelled suddenly, "you were supposed to get off at Exit 32 for Hillcrest."

"Relax." Jake continued his course on the highway. "No one is going to be around at lunchtime. Let's get something to eat first."

The first thought that assailed her when they pulled into the parking lot of the Marketplace Restaurant was that this was the closest thing to a date she'd had with Jake. She began feeling even more on edge than she had in the car. When Jake had surmised that her tension had to do with her being angry about going with him on the calls, he'd only been half right. No, one quarter, she admitted to herself. Three quarters had to do with proximity. His nearness was becoming more and more disconcerting. All the while he was driving, Andy kept sneaking furtive glances at his finely chiseled profile; she was acutely aware of how his gray flannel slacks so clearly outlined the muscles in his powerful thighs; and she knew that he had changed his after-shave. Andy found the new soft lemon scent even more sensual than the musk. She fought off a fantasy or two.

Jake ordered Perrier and lime when the waitress come over to take drink orders. Andy followed suit, throwing him a quizzical look. It was unusual at a business lunch for someone to order a nonalcoholic beverage.

Jake grinned. "That's something else I left out from my life story. I'm a health nut. Once I got serious about my running, I discovered that liquor and exercise don't mix. Except for several cans of beer, of course, to bulk up on carbohydrates before a long race."

"I prefer a large bowl of spaghetti myself." Andy smiled, thinking about the huge carbohydrate feasts she sometimes had with other runners before a meet. Filling up on starches provided needed energy late in the run.

"I must say." Jake laughed. "Sometimes I wonder if I eat to run, or run to eat."

"I know what you mean." Andy grinned. "I don't know where the food goes that I pack away on occasion."

"I don't know either." Jake's brown eyes lingered for a moment over her slender body as he sighed exaggeratedly.

It was the first personal allusion he'd made in days. This time Andy withheld a snappy comeback. She just smiled, her emerald-green eyes sparkling as the sun filtered through the window of the garden restaurant.

Then, embarrassed by Jake's satisfied grin, she quickly asked, "Are you planning to enter any races around here?"

He regarded her with a shocked expression. "What runner ever came to Boston and didn't run the marathon? I figured you knew the course like the back of your hand and would give me some pointers."

"Actually, I just qualified last year," she said defensively. Jake made it sound like the excruciating course of the Boston Marathon was a breeze that a two-year-old could run. It had taken Andy years to build up the stamina even to contemplate the marathon.

"How was it?" he asked with interest.

Again Andy felt defensive. "I had an injury last year and didn't make it for the big event."

"Then we can train together. I still bet you could give me a few pointers, and I might even come up with some myself."

When he saw Andy start to tense, he tousled her hair. "Then again, maybe you already know it all. You do run like a magnificent gazelle."

Andy blushed. It was his first compliment that didn't have heavy overtones of a standard line. "You look quite fleet out there on the track as well."

"My guess is"—he smiled broadly—"that we could be good for each other." He added, "As runners, of course."

Andy told herself it was no big deal that they then made regular plans to run together, but she felt as happy as a kid who'd just been told she could have a candy bar every day.

"I don't know, Mr. Downing," Andy teased flippantly. "First good neighbors, then running partners. What next?"

"Ah, Ms. Howard." He smiled devilishly. "The ball is in your court."

For two supposedly large eaters, neither Andy nor Jake made much of a dent in their chef's salads. An elderly pair from a nearby table who had been watching the younger couple smiled wistfully at each other as Jake took Andy's hand when they left the restaurant.

A time bomb started ticking once they were back in the car and Jake informed Andy that instead of the planned calls, he was going to take her to Rossetti Cosmetics.

"But Rossetti always uses King and Langner to handle their marketing research," Andy explained.

"That's the point," Jake announced. "I intend to go after every account in my territory."

"Jake." Andy's voice grew tense. "Maybe you went around stealing away other companies' accounts in Chicago, but believe me, it's not the thing to do in New England."

"It's the thing to do wherever Jake Downing happens to be." He gave her a self-assured wink.

Andy sat silently fuming for the rest of the drive. But her anger was only a fraction of what she felt a half hour later when she and Jake were introduced to the president of Rossetti's—a statuesque bombshell with flaming red hair, a body that matched Sophia Loren's, and baby-blue eyes that quickly eliminated Andy from the scene, focusing every ounce of attention on the charmingly seductive Mr. Downing.

Andy had to hand it to Jake. He was good, very good. Within minutes he was leaning over Janine Rossetti's shoulder showing her his sales promotion material. And if his words came out a little husky and his breath managed to ruffle the wisps of hair around her ears, Ms. Rossetti did not appear to mind. On the contrary, as Jake displayed his wares, the president in her low-cut V neck Adolfo original amply displayed hers.

While Jake and Janine engaged in their examinations, Andy, feeling painfully dowdy in her conservative blue linen suit, sat across the desk from the pair in utter rage. Not only was he being obnoxiously seductive, but he had purposely invited Andy along to watch. Furthermore, Andy found this kind of underhanded, repulsively chauvinistic style of trying to win accounts completely reprehensible. To her chagrin, Jake got Janine Rossetti to agree to try Horizons' approach for her next line of cosmetics currently in production.

"Well, how did I do?" Jake asked guilelessly when he and Andy got back in the car.

"You are the most despicable, insufferable, ruthless—"

"I gather you don't think too much of my salesmanship." He cut her off, laughing contentedly.

Andy did not say another word the rest of the drive back to the office. Jake switched on the radio to a soft rock station and cheerfully sang along.

CHAPTER FOUR

Andy's running was off again. For two weeks she had put every ounce of strength into her workouts, but she just couldn't seem to get on track. Unfortunately the problem wasn't with her legs; it was with her head. She couldn't concentrate. As soon as she would start to get her pacing smoothed out and her breathing steady, a sensuous image of Jake flitted through her mind, throwing her off. Several times her heart rate started speeding up when she'd catch a glimpse ahead of her of a tall, lanky runner in white. Then she'd spy the runner's face. It was never Jake.

After her rage over the Rossetti affair, Andy told Jake he could forget about their running together. Still, she assumed she would not be able to avoid him at the track. But either Jake had given up running mornings, or else he was braving the city streets.

Andy kept telling herself she couldn't be happier, but she hadn't felt this bad in a long time.

The only occasions Andy seemed to see Jake was at work, and then only in passing. They were both busy. She hadn't gone out on another call with him. She was so angry the day after their first outing that she told Foster that she couldn't spare any more time from her own work to take Jake around. Ted was so elated by Jake's acquisition of the Rossetti account that he didn't argue with her. Andy had the distinct impression that Ted felt confident Jake would do just fine without her introductions.

"Boy, do I love Fridays." Larry sat in Andy's director's chair, one leg dangling over the arm.

As Andy stuck two folders in her atttaché case, she groaned, "Well, my Friday night is taken care of." She patted her case and smirked.

"I'm going to have to start making you go to WA meetings if this keeps up." Larry scowled.

"WA?"

"Workaholics Anonymous—and I fear the disease is progressing." He pursed his lips as he pointed his accusing finger at her.

"You may be right," she agreed with a laugh. "And what's worse, lately I've been getting a driving desire to take the next pile of protocols, chop them up into little pieces, toss them all over Terrible Ted, and start screaming Happy New Year. So what do you think, doc?"

"I already gave you my medical advice ten minutes ago. Come out tonight with me, Tina, and her brother. He's a great guy, and one whiz of a stock-broker. Maybe he'll even have some fabulous ideas about what you can do with all your loot."

"You're an adorable cupid." She grinned, pinching his cheek playfully. "But I'm going to take all my loot, stop at the local Chinese restaurant, take out an extra-large container of Szechwan chicken, and drown myself in paperwork as I slowly die of indigestion."

"Why not ptomaine poisoning while you're at it?"

"Who knows?" Andy grabbed her coat off the rack and waited at the door for Larry to unwrap himself from her chair. "Really, Larry, I appreciate what you're trying to do. But the truth is I just wouldn't be very good company right now." She gave him a friendly peck on the cheek.

"Okay, boss lady, but I still think you'd feel a lot better if you put a little fun into your life." He gave her a friendly squeeze on the shoulder as they walked out the door together.

Once outside Larry walked with Andy as far as the MBTA station. By the time she got to the Chinese restaurant, she had lost her taste for a hot spicy chicken dish after all. She didn't feel particularly hungry for anything. Her chat with Larry came back to haunt her as she walked directly home. She was becoming a workaholic, bringing papers home with her almost every night of the week. And she hadn't done anything for fun for a long time. Working and running took up all her waking hours. And subsequent to that one crazy embrace with Jake, Andy had not gone to a single party or accepted any of the few dates that came her way. She decided despairingly that she was turning into a drab, lackluster person.

Walking into her apartment perked her up a little. It was still her cheerful haven, her place of refuge. For the past few days she'd stopped listening for Jake's footsteps, stopped thinking he'd ask her to walk with him to work, or run with him. She had put the kibosh on all of that. The only thing she couldn't stop was thinking about him. He was outrageous, infuriating, chauvinistic, and condescending. But, she admitted, he was also witty, bright, warm, and even from her brief sampling, she knew he was also a superb lover.

Jake made her feel special. There was just no getting around it. And for all her firm resolution that she would never get involved in a relationship with him, she knew that he nonetheless drove her to distraction, and no other man's image was likely to appear in her fantasies for a long time to come.

Chastising herself for once again letting her thoughts focus on Jake, she flung her attaché case on her couch and went into the bathroom to shower. Feeling refreshed when she finished, she decided to forgo the pile of work she had waiting for her. She went to the phone to call Karen, hoping her friend would want to join her in a movie and a bite to eat. Just as Karen picked up the line, Andy's doorbell rang.

"Hi, Karen, hold on a sec. Someone's at my door." Before Karen answered, Andy set the phone on her end table and dashed out of the room.

There was no one there when she opened the door.

She almost closed it again when her eyes caught something on the floor. Andy bent down a little warily to inspect the large brown paper bag on the doorstep. Cautiously she opened it and peeked in. She did a classic double take. The bag was brimming with grapes. Red and green grapes. Andy glanced up and down the hall, but there was no one around. It was the oddest thing she had ever seen. Bringing them inside her door, she ran back to the phone.

"Sorry," she said, picking up the phone.

"You had me worried there. I was ready to run over and rescue you from some abductor."

"It's really strange," Andy explained, her voice baffled. "Someone left a huge bag of grapes at my door. No note, nothing."

"Maybe it's the Boston Grape Strangler." Karen laughed.

"Well, whoever he is, he's got to be loaded," Andy replied mirthfully. "It's off-season for grapes. They must have cost someone a pretty penny."

"When he shows up, ask him if he has a brother."

"I'm not planning to hang around waiting. Actually, I was calling to see if you felt like a movie or something."

"Gee, I would have loved to, but I promised the folks for three weeks now that I'd come by for dinner tonight. I was just on my way out the door when you called."

"That's okay, we'll go another night," Andy said lightly, hoping to mask her disappointment.

"How about coming home with me? You know

my folks still think of you as one of theirs. We'll just toss an extra plate on the table, and it will be fine."

"Thanks, Karen," Andy said warmly. "I'd enjoy seeing your folks. It has been ages. But I think I'll pass on it tonight."

"Sure," Karen said airily. "Another time."

"Give them an extra kiss for me."

"Will do," Karen chirped. "See you soon."

True to her style, and the reason Andy was so fond of her, Karen never pressed. Their friendship was still as solid as it had been in college. When they hung up, Andy sat on the edge of her bed in her knee-length, soft yellow robe trying to decide whether to get dressed and go out to a show by herself or get into her flannel nightgown and read a long, potboiler in bed for the evening. She'd forgotten all about her cache of grapes until the doorbell rang again.

A little apprehensive, Andy silently fastened the security chain on her door before she asked who was there.

"It is only me, señorita," a voice with a thick Spanish accent answered. "De truck it broke down, and I could not get here sooner." The man's voice then broke into a torrent of garbled Spanish.

Andy opened the door a crack. Jake, arrayed in torn dungarees, a plaid shirt opened to his navel, and bare feet, beamed at her.

"*Buenas noches,* señorita." He smiled disarmingly. "I come to stomp de grapes."

Trying to hold back her laughter, Andy played along. "Where are the rest of you?"

"Ah, señorita, a tragedy has descended on my people—a great god has cursed them with a most devastating disease." He cast his shiny brown eyes down toward the ground and shuffled his feet.

"And just what is this most dread disease?" It was getting harder not to burst into hysterics. Jake was a superbly comic actor, and Andy felt her laughter as well as her heart go out to him.

"It is the dread, the devastating, the horrendous" —the buildup was filled with pathos and suspense— "athlete's foot!"

In that instant Andy knew she was done for. Who could resist an insane comic madman who wooed her with fabulous imitations and bags of grapes. She closed the door to release the security chain.

Partly out of awkwardness, Andy still kept the door ajar and asked, "How do I know you don't have athlete's foot as well? I can't have you stomping all those grapes with diseased toes."

"Ah, señorita," he whispered, his large hand pushing the door open, "I come to bare my soul and my toes to you." The accent faded. Jake stood at the open door gazing at her with a sly twinkle in his eyes.

Andy stepped back from the door, standing aside to let Jake enter. Her knees felt a little weak, and she glanced quickly up at Jake to see if he could hear the loud pounding of her heart.

But Jake, having stepped inside the living room, was taking in the space, curious to learn more about Andy's tastes and interests. "I like it," he said matter-of-factly as he gazed around at the creamy velour sofa and matching armchair, both strewn with gaily

66

colored pillows of every shape and size. A huge wicker trunk served as a coffee table and catchall for various books and magazines. Matisse and Toulouse-Lautrec posters gave the off-white walls both life and warmth.

"I was afraid it might reflect your tough, hard-as-nails, crisp business side. But it doesn't." He turned toward her, and with a soft whisper he added, "This room shows your warm, earthy side."

Andy grinned. "And my sloppy side as well." She picked up a half-knitted sweater from the floor by the couch, tossing it into a wicker basket.

Jake began meandering about, still taking in everything around him. Standing in the middle of the tiny kitchen, he stretched his hands out. They touched the cabinets on both walls. "Let me guess. You don't go in much for cooking."

"I'll have you know," Andy said haughtily as she stepped inside the tight space, "I've made some fabulous Julia Child meals in here."

They were so close they were almost touching. It was Jake who stepped back. He walked into the bedroom. Andy's white towel was strewn across her slightly crumpled bed. She suddenly remembered she was wearing nothing but a thin cotton robe.

One look at Jake's gaze as he glanced from the bed back to her, and she knew he had noticed all too well what she had on. Grinning, she said, *Vamos, amigo,* while I slip on my grape-stomping outfit." Gently she started shoving him toward the door. Jake's hand grabbed hold of the yellow tie around her waist.

"Don't you know that you should never wear

clothes when you make wine? Grape stains never come out." Slowly he began unknotting the tie.

Andy's hands flew up to his. "Jake, don't do this to me. It isn't fair. You told me you wouldn't sit around making plans to seduce me." Her voice was not nearly as strong as she wished.

"It wasn't a plan," he said, his hands disentangling themselves from Andy's, toying now with the open collar of her robe. "I was driven to it. A guy can stand just so much of a gorgeous dame walking all over him."

"Walking all over you." She pulled back in a huff, ready to fight. Fighting with Jake was becoming a regular habit with her.

But Jake pulled her back to him. "Yeah, and my ceiling is about to cave in from those damn clogs of yours."

"Oh, Jake," she flushed, embarrassed at how easily he could get her goat.

His fingers skimmed her throat, lingering on the tiny pulse-beat that was starting to go haywire. Then he moved to her lips. As he gently traced their outline, Andy was conscious of how dry they were. Instinctively her tongue ran over her lips to moisten them, sliding over Jake's finger as well. He tasted good.

Andy could feel the hypnotic spell begin to encompass her. As Jake placed his enticing hands on her temples, the light pressure made her feel as though she was floating. With infinite tenderness he started to kiss her—first her eyes, then her cheeks, the tip of her nose, her earlobes. Andy began to desperately long for him to kiss her again the way he did that day on the track. She lifted her lips to him, parting them in anticipation. But Jake only kissed her offered lips in the same light, tender way.

This time when his hands went to the tie of her robe, Andy's hands didn't follow. They were too busy gliding over the tight, curly hairs of his chest. The knot easily undone, Jake slipped his warm hands inside the robe. That first magical moment when he touched her soft, yielding flesh was unbelievably wonderful. The pressure intensified ever so slightly as he began to explore the curves of her athletically firm body. Still he left the robe in place, as though to postpone the sweet glory of her nakedness.

Andy placed her lips on his neck, planting tiny kisses down his throat and then his hard, firm chest. As the pressure of his hands increased on her soft, pliant body, Andy's kisses grew more fierce and passionate. Her hands tugged at Jake's open shirt, pulling it out of the waistband of his tight dungarees. He dropped his hands away from her body for the instant it took him to let his shirt slide off. Then opening the soft folds of her robe, he enveloped her, crushing her to him with a husky groan of pleasure.

At last, as his lips urgently captured hers, he slid her robe off her shoulders, letting it fall softly to the floor.

"Oh, Jake," Andy murmured as their kiss finally ended, and Jake gazed down with infinite longing at her slender form. "I'm sinking fast." Her sultry voice was hot with desire. But there was a hint of fear in her words as well. She wanted him desperately, but even now there was that dot of rational thought, that nagging realization that she had sworn not to let this happen. The problem was she knew she didn't have the control to stop. The erotic sensations were fast drowning her.

They tumbled together, arms interlocked around one another, onto the bed. Again his mouth found hers, his fingers tangling around her auburn curls. His lips moved to her neck, then slowly, lovingly edged down to the tender valley between her breasts. His hands caressed her face, his fingers gently tracing a line from the bridge of her nose to her cheeks. A tear lightly splashed on his skin.

Jake suddenly backed off. His eyes traveled from her soft, beautiful body to her face. Her eyes reflected passion and desire, but there was no denying the sprinkle of tears, the ambivalence her mind was struggling with despite her body's longing.

"I want you badly, Andy. I can't remember wanting anyone as much as I want you."

Andy put her arms lightly around Jake and kissed the tip of his nose, then she eased away from him, looking him straight in the eye, completely comfortable in her nakedness.

"You drive me wild, you know. But not only with desire." She smiled impishly, her eyes still watery from her unshed tears. "I can't remember getting so angry at any man. Why the hell couldn't you have been a car salesman or a—a bill collector even. Anything but the sales coordinator for my company. Mine. And you're moving in with bombs bursting, flags flying. Damn you, you're taking Horizons by storm, and"—she gave him a sheepish look—"I hate you for it." She turned away and then swung back. "And besides all of that, you'll probably run the marathon in record time while I make it to the finish line last and on my knees." She sat up on the bed, resting her elbows on her thighs, her hands cupping her chin.

Jake moved closer to her, stroking her back in a light, comforting way. "I wish I was a car salesman at this moment, and one that limped badly besides. Poor Andy, you make everything a competition. I don't want to compete with you. I know I can easily get you into bed, but I'm not willing to have you blame me for seducing you." Kissing her gently on the cheek, he said, "Come on. Get dressed. We've got a lot of grapes to crush." He stood up and walked over to the door. Pausing, he looked back at her. "If you help me stomp enough for one bottle of wine, I'll even treat you to dinner."

As he started out the door, Andy's quietly timid voice stopped him. "I've been wanting to ask you. How did you get that scar by your mouth?"

He touched his finger to the tiny half-moon line and grinned at her. "That's from my days as an Indy 500 race car driver. Just as I was coming in first at the finish line, some blond bombshell leaned over the railing, and I went into a tailspin. And now I bear this reminder," he declared, tapping the scar, "to keep my eyes on the road."

Andy tossed her pillow at him as he sprinted out of the room.

* * *

71

Saturday morning Andy woke up with a hangover. Rubbing her throbbing temples, she tried to recall just how many glasses of Chianti she had consumed the evening before. For a pair who rarely drank, Jake and Andy had seen at least two bottles of the hearty red Burgundy disappear last night—along with overflowing platefuls of spaghetti carbonara. They had dined in the North End, the renowned Italian section of Boston, at a small, street-front restaurant, Mother Anna's.

Andy's fingers instinctively moved to her lips as she lay in bed. The memory of Jake's good night kiss still lingered. When he walked Andy to her door last night, he tousled her hair affectionately, kissed her lightly, and informed her he'd better leave quickly or he wouldn't be held accountable for the results.

As Andy stretched her arm out across the empty space beside her on the bed, she knew Jake was right. It would have taken very little for them to have ended up together for the night. One good night kiss had not satisfied either one of them.

She was playing with fire, and she knew the outcome. She was going to get burned. Last night she had almost leaped into the flames, a willing victim. How many more times could she tamper with the fates?

It was an awful dilemma. When she refused to have anything to do with him, she was miserable, and when she was with him, she did nothing but worry. They had agreed to a casual friendship. They would walk to work together, run together, maybe even have dinner together on occasion. When Andy kept pointing out to Jake last night that even a casual involvement really went against her principles, he teasingly accused her of being prejudiced. If he were a woman co-worker whom she liked, he claimed, she wouldn't have any qualms about their friendly involvement.

Who were they fooling? It wasn't a casual friend who had slipped that robe off her shoulders last night, and she did not feel the least bit casual about her fierce desire to have him make love to her. How many more times was she really going to be able to pull back? And even if she could, it didn't change the fact that she longed for someone she knew would ultimately hurt her professionally and probably emotionally as well.

She no longer believed that she was simply an obstacle that Jake was trying to seductively coerce. There was no doubt in her mind that he was very attracted to her. But she was convinced that Jake saw her as a challenge, and she was certain that he was the kind of man who loved a good challenge. He had made it clear from the start that he was unattached and unencumbered. The message Andy heard was that he liked it that way. Every ounce of common sense that Andy had accrued over the years told her to call the whole thing off—now. Squinting at her tableside alarm clock, she saw it was after seven A.M. Jake had told her he'd pick her up around nine A.M. He was going to show her "what a real workout is like."

She wondered if he would be awake yet. She had a desperate need to call him now while she felt charged up with the courage to back out of the whole thing. For a few moments she practiced some lines. "I don't want anything to do with you"—no, that was too hostile. "Let's keep our friendship strictly at work"—no, even that was more than she could handle. "I'm afraid I'm falling in love with you, Jake Downing, and there's no way I'm going to let that happen to me." That was the honest truth, and she could barely bring herself to acknowledge it, much less say it out loud to Jake. That was all he would need to hear. He would have her just where he wanted her, and in no time she would be a goner. She remembered how long it had taken her to forgive herself for her naïveté about Ken. What excuse could she give herself this time? How many times, she scolded herself, do I have to get burned before I stop sticking my hand in the fire?

She got as far as calling information and getting Jake's number, but she never marked it down.

At nine sharp Jake rapped lightly on her door. Andy's headache felt worse as she went to let him in. The pain at this point had less to do with the wine and more to do with the last two hours she'd spent chastising herself for cowardice. Jake's vibrant face and surging energy, as he stood there looking so vigorous in his gray sweat suit, made her feel even worse.

"Jake, I feel rotten," Andy confessed. "Why don't you go ahead and do your workout without me today."

"Oh, no. You're not getting off so easy," he declared, steering her to the sofa. "Show daddy where it hurts."

As if she were a child, she pointed poutingly to her head. Jake sat her down and began slowly to massage her temples. Andy sighed aloud at the contact of his cool fingers on her skin. But then she remembered where Jake's massages had led last time.

Standing up abruptly, she said, "Oh, no. That's part of what gave me the headache in the first place."

"My massage?" he said, puzzled.

Andy started to pace around the room. "I've been trying to get myself to call you all morning. If I could magically make you disappear—vanish like a puff of smoke—I'd do it. My problem is I stink at magic." She sat down on the armchair, one hand on each temple, her elbows perched on the arms of the seat. "I don't think this awful headache is going to go away until you get out of my life."

Jake walked over to her seat. Bending down on his knees, so they were eye to eye, he took her hands away from her head, holding them down on her knees.

"I'm not the one hurting your head—you are. You work so hard at denying your feelings that it's no wonder your head throbs. Look, Andy, you don't need to perform magic to make me vanish. I'll walk out that door right now; I'll look the other way every time we pass at work, or on the track; I'll make believe we aren't wildly attracted to each other—if that's really what you want. So, if you'd rather have your life neatly cordoned off into safe little sections,

75 .

never letting them mix, then I'm going to have to live with that."

For several seconds they looked intensely at one another. Neither of them spoke. Finally, with a heavy sigh, Jake stood up and walked slowly to the door.

He turned the doorknob and started to leave the room.

"Jake, wait." He turned around.

She told herself she was crazy. He was offering her the magic that she wanted. She told herself a lot of things. But she grabbed her jacket, flinging it over her sweat suit, and ran to catch hold of his outstretched hand.

CHAPTER FIVE

"I can't—do it," Andy groaned.

"Sure you can. Just one more," Jake coaxed.

Sweat was pouring profusely down Andy's face. Her tee shirt was drenched. Andy was convinced as she sat strapped into the black vinyl and steel contraption resembling something from the dark ages that she would rather die than lift the metal bar one more time.

Every muscle in her body cried for mercy. For the past hour Jake had put Andy through what she described as torture only befitting a murderer from Devil's Island. Andy had heard about Nautilus gymnasiums before. Many runners extolled the virtues of the rigorous workout that required using a series of machines operated on a weighted pulley system. As the body built up muscular strength, the weights were added to constantly force the muscles to work harder.

What Andy didn't know was how excruciatingly hard it was going to be. When she first walked in, her only concern was whether she would be able to exercise in the midst of at least twenty body-beautiful men, all of whom were strapped to an assortment of machines, grunting and groaning through their reps in the dark, pungent-smelling basement torture chamber. The only other sound was the cacophonous noise of metal crashing.

She needn't have worried about the men making her feel self-conscious. No one even looked up when Jake started her on the first machine—a calf exerciser. And as Jake increased the weights, forcing Andy to use every ounce of strength she possessed, she immediately understood why none of the men even knew she existed. When you lifted weights, nothing else mattered but hoisting those bars.

"No more, I'm begging you," Andy gasped. Her upper arms were pressed against the leather pads of the biceps machine.

"Push," Jake demanded. "Pain for gain, Andy. That's the saying here."

"What about the saying It's not worth dying over."

"Last one, I promise." Jake laughed. "Then I'll let you die in peace."

He stepped behind her, his damp chest pressed against her drenched back. His arms around her, he placed his hands under hers.

"Come on, baby, I'll even help you." He whispered the words hoarsely in her ear, sending a shiver of earthy physical awareness down her spine.

Andy took in a deep breath. Gathering up the last dregs of energy she possessed, arms trembling, and with Jake's support, she pushed the bar out one last time. As Jake unstrapped her, she fell into his arms, gasping. He held her caressingly as she fought to catch her breath. With his arms still encircling her, he asked, grinning, "So what do you think of my workout program?"

"If I had the strength to lift a knife right now, I'd show you what I think of your medieval horror house." Then looking up at him, she laughed. "Actually, if I can live through it, I'm going to be so strong I'll be able to fly across that finish line."

"You will, I promise," Jake agreed. "But right now, lady, you need a long, hot shower and some rest."

"It isn't fair." Andy snickered. "I'm a washed-out rag ready to be tossed away, and except for a little healthy sweat, you look terrific."

"I know it's hard to believe, but it does get easier." Jake laughed. "Don't get me wrong. If it doesn't hurt and those muscles don't start throbbing, then you're wasting your time."

"I know, I know." Andy mimicked Jake's husky voice now. "Pain for gain. That's one I'm not likely to forget."

The stinging hot shower helped. The women's locker room left something to be desired, but Andy was glad to see several other women had come into the place. She guessed from their general appearance, especially their well-muscled legs, that a few of them must be runners too. As painful as she had found the exercises, she was grateful to Jake for indoctrinating her. Her modest home workout was obviously no comparison to the toughening and strengthening exercises that the Nautilus equipment provided.

As exhausted as she felt, there was also a feeling of exhilaration. The exercises were partly responsible, but all during the workout Andy had been acutely aware of Jake's presence, and not only in a physical sense. There was an aura of sensuality about him that kept transmitting itself to Andy. His subtle touches, the way he spoke to her, those emotion-laden brown eyes, and especially that sexy smile made particularly virile by the half-moon scar—every aspect of this man excited and stimulated her. She had never met anyone like Jake before. A part of her kept saying—"Go for it, you fool. Forget all your fears and insecurities. He's right for you." But still that other voice overlaid the first. It was a voice of warning. "This will never work. And when it ends, what then?"

Andy fell asleep as Jake drove home in her old VW bug. The next thing she knew she was being carried up the stairs of her apartment house. She felt like dead weight in Jake's arms, and she didn't make one peep of protest for him to put her down. Besides being exhausted, it felt good to be held.

"Okay, madame," Jake declared, setting her upright at her door. "Taxi service ends here. You may be a luscious number, love, but you are no light-weight."

"Pain for gain, remember." Andy chuckled.

"I think we've both gained enough for one day."

"I couldn't agree more," Andy said, handing Jake her key. As he opened the door, she let out an indiscreet yawn. Smiling sleepily, she walked inside.

"Go get some more shut-eye," he ordered, pushing her toward the bedroom.

Andy threw him a quizzical look.

"You sleep, I'll cook." He smiled. "Unless, of course, you want a little rubdown first."

With a grin, Andy said, "Let's see about your culinary skills. I already know your talent as a masseur."

"Well, I don't promise anything." Jake began checking out the contents of one of the cupboards. He had to lean back for the door to swing open. "I've never had to cook in a closet before," he teased.

"No excuses," Andy yelled out behind her closed door. "I'm only going to rest for a few minutes, and when I get up, I want a feast fit for—ouch."

"Problem?" Jake shouted back.

"Not unless having every single fiber of your body feel like it is coming unglued is a problem. Are you sure this wasn't some diabolical plot of yours to do away with me so you could get my apartment as well as my job?"

Jake opened the door. His eyes were warm and serious as he gazed at her on the bed. "It's you I want, my delectable complainer, not your apartment." For a moment the room was charged with an

81

electric stillness as they both eyed each other. Then Jake smiled impishly. "Although I wouldn't argue if you wanted to share your place with me as well."

"I think you've moved in on me enough for the moment," Andy murmured, not taking her eyes off him. "How about that masterful lunch you were supposed to whip up?"

Jake grinned, but made no effort to move. Andy knew that if he started toward her, she would not be able to stop him. Maybe it was cowardly to let herself be led into this relationship by Jake, but she had reached the point where it was no longer possible for her to honestly tell him to keep away. She wanted him too much.

The phone rang. It settled any decision either of them might have made. Andy picked up the receiver as Jake quietly shut the door and went back to the kitchen.

Andy's voice cracked as she said hello.

"Don't tell me I woke you up at 11:30," Karen exclaimed. "That would be a first."

"I haven't been sleeping, just dying," Andy groaned dramatically. "I've been out all morning learning what a workout is all about."

"You and your exercises," Karen teased. "One of these days I'm going to have to teach you the joys of indolent bliss."

"Right now nothing could sound better." Andy sighed as she stretched out on the bed.

"Well, believe it or not, I have something even better to offer today," Karen declared enthusiastically. "How would you like a luscious dinner tonight at Maître Jacques?"

"My, my, did you win the state lottery?" Andy exclaimed. Her pocketbook didn't allow too many fifty-dollar-a-person dinners.

"Almost. I won the heart of a dashing young executive from Mason and Reynold's, one of our law firm accounts."

"And you need a chaperon?" Andy teased.

"No. I need a best friend for his old college buddy from New York who's in town on business."

"You know me and blind dates," Andy moaned, adding with a good-natured laugh, "Only the fact that I love you like a sister made me agree to those previous finds of yours."

"Well this one—believe it or not—is fabulous-looking and wealthy. I already checked him out."

"He must have a fatal flaw," Andy insisted, laughing. "But the ideal man or not—I can't tonight. I'm about to ask someone to dinner."

"So you've been holding out on me. Who's the mystery man?"

"I'll tell you about it some other time."

"He must be pretty special to turn down Maître Jacques."

Jake walked into the room carrying a tray of sandwiches. He set them on the bed and sat down beside her, stretching his long torso next to her. "Lunch is served, love," he whispered loudly in her ear.

"Sounds like you're already occupied." Karen chuckled. "You better go—eat. Talk to you later."

When Andy hung up the receiver, she grimaced at Jake. "You did that on purpose."

"You object to friends knowing you lunch in bed with your cook?" Perfectly at ease, he readjusted the pillow behind his head and took a grilled cheese sandwich from the tray.

"What am I going to do about you?"

"I can tell you in just a few words." Jake smiled. The banter was light and playful as they ate the sandwiches and drank the somewhat stale wine from Andy's refrigerator. Andy tried unsuccessfully to act cool and natural, even though she and Jake were sharing her bed. She had completely lost her appetite —for lunch. She placed her barely eaten sandwich back on the plate. Jake didn't say a word. He took the tray off the bed, setting it on the end table.

When he returned to stretch out next to her, Andy's body turned perceptibly toward him. Jake picked up the subtle nuance of her move. Slipping his arm under her, he curled her body against him.

"Is the battle over?" he whispered into the silken strands of her hair as she rested her head on his shoulder. His fingers tenderly caressed her neck. Beyond that he made no move. He seemed to be waiting for Andy's decision.

The air was charged with an electrical current. Andy paused for a few moments, vaguely aware of her trembling body. Then, pulling him gently toward her, she brushed her lips against his ear. In a low, throaty voice, she whispered, "Something tells me the battle has just begun."

84

"Uh, uh," he uttered, in between tiny, nibbling kisses. "Let's make love, not war."

When his lips found hers, she found herself letting go at last. This was the man she wanted. Every fiber of her being reached out to him. His warm, sensuous mouth felt so right, so natural. Arching toward him in an almost feline pose, she sighed at how perfectly she fit against him. Jake's tongue probed deeper into her mouth, his hands moving with slow deliberation like a sculptor lovingly caressing his creation.

Andy waited breathlessly for Jake to begin to undress her. Their clothing felt like such a barrier. For a moment she contemplated taking the initiative but decided to let Jake set the pace.

She was consumed with the desire to feel his hard, muscled flesh, to learn the magnificent contours of his body, to make them her own. In an impatient gesture, she slipped her hands up under his shirt, her fingers tracing a tremulous line against the waistband of his pants. Jake softly crooned his pleasure, but still languidly continued his teasing, tantalizing explorations without making any attempt to remove her clothes. His gleaming eyes told her he knew exactly what he was doing. He was intentionally heightening her torment, her desire. As her body instinctively writhed in response to his skillful embraces, Jake remained masterfully in control.

Finally, unable to hold back her need, Andy moaned, "Don't you think we would be more comfortable if you took this off?" She tugged at the collar of his turtleneck.

"Still trying to take charge." He grinned seductively, his fingers lingering on her still-covered breast, toying with her nipples in an idle caress that was driving Andy wild with an excruciating combination of passion and frustration.

Biting his ear hard enough for him to groan, Andy hissed, "You like me this way, don't you? Begging for you, pleading with you to strip me bare, wanting you to take me so badly I could scream."

"I've just been waiting to bring out the wanton vixen in you. I love it when you're uninhibited. Those low, throaty moans of pleasure, those trembling shivers you transmit. I want to hear how much you want me. I want you to show me how much."

Jake slid off of her, rolling over to his side, poised in leisurely anticipation. He had chided her for taking charge, and now he was telling her to take the lead with full reins. A flash of anger shot through her—or was it embarrassment that stung. Andy was not a novice at lovemaking, but it was one area where she always followed the man's lead. Jake was different. But then, of course, he would be.

Suddenly Andy grinned at him. "So you want me to play leader, do you? You may regret this." She eyed him with a mischievous smile. Rolling away from him, she slid off the bed. Jake rolled flat on his back, his head comfortably resting on two pillows. His dark brown eyes watched Andy glide over to her bureau. With one hand she flicked on her radio—soft jazz music filling the room. With slow deliberation, her sparkling green cat eyes honed in on Jake's slightly parted lips, she sidled back to him. Standing almost on top of him, she began to painstakingly unsnap the row of metal closures down her sweat suit jacket. She had nothing on under it. After her workout this morning she had slipped her bra and soaked tee shirt into her duffel bag. Likewise her panties and shorts. The feel of the soft cotton velour of her outfit against her freshly showered skin had felt deliciously naughty. She realized now that her decision to be with Jake had really been made back at the gym.

Jake watched, his chest heaving deeply, as Andy, undulating provocatively to the music, slipped off the jacket. When Jake's hand reached up to touch her, she scooted out of his reach with a taunting grin. "Oh, no Jake—not yet."

He laughed, enjoying her display of exhibitionism with gleeful delight. Andy too was beginning to get into it more fully. At first she simply had meant to tantalize Jake as he had her, forcing him to admit his unbridled, impatient lust. But now Andy found herself getting wrapped up in her carefree abandon. Alluringly, her sweat pants still on, she half sat, half perched on Jake's lap. He had changed after their workout into a turtleneck shirt and dungarees. Andy ran her fingers down his chest, and then slowly began edging the shirt up. Jake obliged her by lifting his back slightly off the bed so that she could slip the turtleneck over his head. Her long slender fingers slid through his mussed hair, her naked breasts in the process skimming lightly against his chest. It felt so deliciously sensual, Andy did it again, this time planting a dozen kisses on his neck and throat. Jake groaned loudly, his hands reaching up to the waistband of Andy's pants. Andy placed her own hands on top of his, preventing him from wandering. Her movement had the effect of causing her firm, ripe breasts to edge further to Jake's lips. With his shielded hands he pressed her waist tightly, his mouth lifting up to grasp one taut nipple between his lips.

"Not fair," Andy quipped with a sigh of delight, but she didn't move away. Instead, she guided Jake's hands up her rib cage cupping each of them around her breasts.

"You have the most delectable, velvety soft breasts," he murmured as he caressed her, tenderly at first, and then, inhaling sharply, the pressure became more demanding, more urgent. Sitting on his lap, Andy was very aware of his mounting need. As he began to draw her to him, Andy planted her hands firmly on the bed at either side of his shoulders, preventing herself from falling onto him.

With a devilish glint in her eye, she whispered, "First tell me how much you want me. I want to know if I drive you crazy with desire."

"I give." He grinned, a guttural sigh escaping his lips. "I almost forgot, in the heat of passion, what a determined little competitor you are. Okay, you win. Gladly." He put his arms around her, his hands tugging at her waistband, his tongue darting out to her erect nipples.

Her hands drew him away from her breast, forcing his hungry eyes to her own.

"Well?" she purred tauntingly.

"Okay, if I can't have you this moment, I will go mad. I'm begging you to let me make love to you." With each word, he tugged her pants down further.

Andy made no move to stop him. Instead, as he reached her ankles, she rolled off him onto the bed so he could slip the pants off completely. He gazed longingly at her as he swiftly unbuckled his belt. Quickly unzipping his dungarees, he wriggled out of them. Andy felt a pulsating excitement as she gazed admiringly at his magnificent physique.

The fun and games were over. As Jake rejoined Andy on the bed, he pulled her fiercely to him.

"You're beautiful," he whispered. "You feel so good."

Andy surrendered herself to his exploring hands as they traced her curving form, each touch binding her to him. She, too, boldly reached out to discover every line, every muscle of his body. Jake's mouth sought hers in a hungry quest to possess her lips. His mouth never leaving hers, his hands continued to entice her with an intimacy that dispelled all other thought.

In tantalizing strokes he ran his fingers over her flat abdomen down to the satiny softness of her thighs. When his lips followed the path his hands had blazed, Andy cried out with a gasp. "Please, Jake. Please." Her fingertips pressed fiercely into his shoulders. She planted hungry kisses down his chest, her tongue tasting the delicious saltiness of his moist skin.

"My beautiful, intoxicating vixen," Jake whispered as he drew atop Andy for their long-desired union. She gasped with rapturous pleasure as he slipped inside of her. Moving together in sublime union, totally in tune with each other, their pace steadily quickened as their passion grew more intense. Reaching the peak of ecstasy at exactly the same moment, their minds and bodies surrendered fully to the ultimate experience, crying out in mutual abandon.

Never had Andy imagined lovemaking could be this enchanting and wondrous. Never had she felt such a psychic oneness with anyone. Jake filled her with an exquisite sense of fulfillment that went beyond the purely physical. That she loved him she already knew; but that she was capable of so openly giving her love amazed her. He had unlocked a passion inside of her that had never before been tapped.

Even as the sensation of fiery passion began to ebb, Andy loved the wonderful, luxuriating feeling of Jake's caressing hands lightly stroking her. Idly, she ran her fingers down his chest. Jake pulled her closer to him, planting tiny kisses on her forehead.

"You do magical things to me, Jake Downing," she said aloud, nestling into the warmth of his chest and inhaling the musky love-scent of his body with satisfied delight.

"It's about time." He swept her dampened hair away from her neck and kissed her moist forehead lightly. "I was afraid for a while that I was going to end up a flop as a magician. You can't guess at the number of spells I've been weaving since I set eyes on you."

"And now that the spell has finally worked?" She lifted her head up level to his.

"I still have quite a bit of magic up my sleeve," he teased, yawning.

It was contagious. Andy too stretched out and yawned.

"I think we're both worn out. Maybe we took on too much of a workout," Jake said, that crooked smile of his slanting his half-moon scar.

"And I was just getting the hang of it, too," Andy replied drolly.

"I promise, love, to give you more practice later tonight. Say around eleven."

"Eleven." Andy grimaced. "I was planning on proving to you at dinner tonight just what kind of fabulous meal could be whipped up in my little closet kitchen." There was a sinking sensation that crept in unbidden. "What's the matter with tonight?"

"Tonight, beautiful, I'm afraid it's business before pleasure," Jake answered nonchalantly as he stood and slipped on his dungarees.

"Business? I hadn't heard of any sales meetings for this evening."

Jake walked up to her, planting a feather-light kiss on her cheek. "I guess that means you're just not privy to everything that goes on in the sales department. It happens that Ms. Rossetti has asked me to a business dinner tonight—to go over my—"

She didn't listen to him finish. Storming over to her closet for her robe, she reeled around to him. "Isn't that cozy for you. Now you can sample the enchanting Ms. Rossetti's exercise program."

"Calm down, tiger," Jake said silkily. "I told you it was business."

"Business, is it," Andy spat out, her face burning with a flushed rage. "And who better than I knows

91

how you love to mix business with pleasure? I must have been crazy to fall for your . . . your . . ."

"Spell?" Jake offered, laughing.

"I am not amused," Andy said haughtily, pulling the tie of her robe tight. Inside she felt as though her world was coming apart at the seams, but she was damned if she was going to give Jake even an inkling of the pain she felt.

"I think I love you better when you're lusty than when you're jealous." Jake grinned as he attempted to kiss her.

"It is not jealousy. It's fury—fury at my own stupidity," Andy stormed as she reeled away from his touch.

"Let's discuss it later tonight," Jake said, some of his own irritation surfacing in his low tone.

"There is not going to be any later. Why don't you just chalk one up as your win and forget it. I just remembered I have a dinner invitation that I want to get ready for. So please leave."

"Fickle, too." Jake grinned, convinced Andy's date was an invention to save face.

Andy knew full well what he thought. Walking over to the door of her room, she opened it for Jake. "If you happen to start off your little business get-together at Maître Jacques, don't feel obliged to greet me." She stood, arms on her hips, impatiently tapping her foot.

Jake, sighing, started toward the door. He paused as he reached her side. "Andy, it's really too bad you don't trust me. I don't particularly go for one-night stands. We're just going to have to find a spell for those suspicious little thoughts of yours."

Andy knew if she said too much more she would start to lose control and break down. That Jake wanted her to believe that he would spent a purely business evening with the lusciously attractive Janine Rossetti was laughable. Andy had already seen him lay the groundwork for his seduction of the cosmetics queen.

"Save your spells for your other conquests," Andy said icily.

Jake opened his mouth to say something, but he could see the shield descend over Andy's eyes. He knew it was going to be futile to try to get through to her right now. Sighing with weary resignation, he shrugged his shoulders and walked out.

CHAPTER SIX

Andy sat back on her heels dangling the errant black leather pump in her hand. Flushed with the exertion of scrambling around the cluttered floor of her closet for the past ten minutes, she felt triumphant. Well at least something had gone right today. She stood up, promptly stepping into her shoes and then gathering her dress up from the bed.

She had bought the dress weeks ago on an impulse. It was shortly after Jake had put her down for her businesslike appearance. This little number was far from staid. The soft chocolate-brown silk material clung in all the right places, draping around Andy's tall, lithe body like it was a part of her. The low-cut, revealing bodice made her hesitate about wearing it—only for a moment. Then with renewed determination she set about pinning her hair in a sophisticated chignon, letting a few tendrils dangle provocatively around her face and neck.

Checking her outfit in the mirror, she smiled with satisfaction. Only when she looked back at her face was she forced to confront the hollow emptiness reflected in the glass. At least her eyes were no longer red and swollen, she thought with relief, trying to buoy her spirits. The improvement was minimal at best—her face was pale, for all the costly surface adornment.

When Jake walked out the door that afternoon, Andy fell apart. That unbelievable high she had experienced making love to him fell crashing down on her like an avalanche. After the flood of tears came her rage—more at herself than Jake. She had pegged him right from the beginning. He was a big-town hotshot who knew what he wanted and used any means to acquire it. So if it meant slipping in and out of women's beds, Andy recognized now that Jake would have no qualms about it whatsoever. She had feared the worst, and it was all happening.

The problem was she had started to fall in love with him. And once on that ride she couldn't get off. Jake had been in the driver's seat all along, and as much as she had fussed and fumed about not liking where he was leading her, she had never honestly asked him to stop and let her out.

This time it was a lot worse than when she bid her adieus to Ken. She had been so young and impressionable then. What she took for love she later came to see was infatuation. There was no doubt in her mind about Jake. Now the only issue was how she was going to cope with the bitter emptiness left in his wake.

Andy had already decided on her first step. Again she studied her image in the mirror, forcing a smile onto her face. A little more makeup was definitely in order. So what if it took some extra help from Revlon to give her face that bright, alive look which Jake had brought out with no blusher at all. She was determined to look good, even if it was only skin-deep.

Maître Jacques was one of Andy's favorite restaurants. The large, elegant room was dotted with white-clothed tables arranged amidst lush fern planters. Each table was adorned with a graceful silver bud vase holding a single red rose. The whole mood of the place was one of simple, understated sophistication.

Andy watched the waiter clear away her plate of half-eaten veal chasseur. The delicate white asparagus accompanying the succulent meat hadn't even been sampled. She had no appetite, having eaten only enough to appear politely appreciative. After all, her dinner had cost a pretty penny, and her date seemed like a perfectly nice guy. Andy was thankful that Daniel was also quite talkative. Karen and the two men kept up a steady, gregarious conversation throughout the meal, allowing Andy to remain relatively quiet.

"Come on, Andy. Have at least a bite of the soufflé." Daniel held a teaspoon in front of her lips. Maître Jacques was famous for their chocolate soufflé, and Andy usually adored it. Tonight, the overly rich aroma simply made her stomach feel queasy.

"No thanks. Honestly, I'm just not terribly hungry tonight." She lifted her barely touched coffee to her lips, thankful that the dinner was almost over. Karen caught her eye from across the table, a supportive smile on her lips. Even though Andy had said nothing about why she had decided to accept Karen's offer of the double date tonight, her friend's smile expressed an unspoken understanding.

Andy had to give Karen credit. She had been right about Daniel Reed. Her date was attractive, intelligent, and charmingly attentive. For the past two hours he painstakingly sought to draw Andy out. She did make an effort to be cordial and involved, but it was almost impossible for her to keep her attention focused on the evening at hand. She was amazed that Daniel hadn't given up by now. Maybe, she decided, he was so unused to a woman not falling all over him that she presented a pleasant challenge. If so, his plan was lost on Andy.

She couldn't stop thinking about Jake, nor could she erase the remnants of their passionate lovemaking. His touch had left a permanent mark. His lips and hands had claimed her. She could still feel his embraces and remember her own abandon—the ecstasy that had erupted for both of them. She loved him. And she hated him.

Images of Jake and Janine Rossetti kept insidiously flashing across Andy's mind. The worst part, Andy thought bitterly, was his casual attitude about the whole thing. He was not only a philanderer but

97

perfectly at ease about being one. That he could jump so easily from her loving arms to another woman made Andy see red. And worse, it hurt with a gnawing ache that wouldn't let up.

"How about letting me share your little daydream?" Daniel's deep baritone voice and the light touch of his hand on her forearm startled her out of her thoughts.

"Sorry. I am rather preoccupied tonight. About work," she quickly added. "It would seem very boring to an outsider," she blurted out, immediately realizing how rude she had inadvertently sounded. Her usually skilled repartee with dates, even ones she was not particularly interested in, had totally abandoned her tonight. Afraid of putting her foot in her mouth further, she opted for a warm and friendly smile instead.

Daniel smiled back, taking hold of Andy's hand. "I never did like being left out in the cold. I guess I'm just going to have to find some way to become an insider. Tell me, what's the magic word?"

"I'm afraid I just don't believe in magic," Andy said tightly. She felt a sinking regret for having come here tonight. It was unfair to all of them. Her mood was depressingly low, her interest in flirtatious small talk nil. She had a strong desire to crawl into bed and cry herself to sleep. Quietly, she excused herself and went off to the ladies' room.

Heedless of the two women refreshing their makeup and combing their hair, Andy sat down at a vacant chair, bleakly staring at her reflection in the mirror and watching the tears begin to well up in the

98

corners of her eyes, slowly, relentlessly rolling down her cheeks. She was oblivious to the surreptitious stares of the other women before they walked back out and didn't even notice Karen pull up a chair next to her.

"Tell sis all about it," Karen ordered softly, putting her arm comfortingly around her friend.

"Damn him, damn him, damn him," Andy muttered hoarsely. She still looked straight into the mirror, but her eyes, blurred with tears, didn't really see anything.

"What do we have here—a broken record?" Karen cajoled, squeezing Andy's shoulder.

Despite herself, Andy laughed. "Look at me—will you? I am a mature, sophisticated, independent woman. And I'm out tonight with a perfectly delightful man who has been falling all over me the entire evening."

"So far, correct." Karen grinned. Small and dark-haired, she looked particularly impish right now. "When do we get to the bad part?"

Ignoring her question, Andy pulled a tissue from her leather clutch bag, and after trying in vain to erase the smudged mascara, she blew her nose soundly.

"That bastard has reduced me to a blithering idiot." Andy smiled damply at her friend.

"I take it 'that bastard' refers to the mystery man of this afternoon who obviously was otherwise occupied for dinner this evening."

"Very occupied." Andy snickered. Regarding

Karen with a baleful expression, she added, "And I hate to tell you who the mystery man is."

"Let me guess," Karen interjected. "Is it none other than the dastardly Jake Downing, usurper of your sought-after position at Horizons, and"—she grinned devilishly—"usurper of some other things as well?"

"That obvious, huh?"

"You know good old Shakespeare—'The lady doth protest too much.' " Karen eyed Andy with a knowing smile.

Andy had blown off steam about Jake to Karen several times. She smiled through her tears at her perceptive friend. The smile quickly became transformed into a frown. "What makes me so mad, so mad I could scream, is that I fell for the whole thing, lock, stock, and barrel. Oh, I was tough for a while there. I put up just enough of a fight to satisfy my—my 'outmoded sense of business ethics,' as Jake so charmingly put it. But he had me the whole time, and he knew it. And I knew it. So I told myself to stop worrying, to reach out for what I wanted so badly, and most important—to trust him." She put her hands up to her throbbing head, massaging her pulsating temples.

"My head is killing me, I've got this miserable ringing in my ears, and I think I just got a run in my panty hose. I'm falling apart," she moaned, a weak smile softening her despairing sigh.

"It sounds like love to me," Karen offered with a teasing nudge to Andy's shoulder.

"Love!" Andy sputtered. "You think I love a conniving, deceitful, fickle . . . You're right, I love him," she admitted deflatedly.

Leaving out the intimate preliminaries, Andy told Karen about Jake's dinner engagement with Janine Rossetti.

With a sympathetic smile, Karen said, "You know, Andy, it is possible that the guy is on the level. Maybe it really was strictly business."

Andy gave her a disparaging nod. "You are as gullible as Jake was hoping I would be. And you've never set your eyes on Janine Rossetti. She makes the *Playboy* pinups look underdeveloped. No, Karen. Jake's sense of fidelity is nonexistent. I'm just going to have to grit my teeth through the pain and try to exorcise him."

"Well, if you need any help, I could always dig up my old voodoo doll and stick some pins in it."

"Start sticking!" Andy grinned through her tears.

The cab pulled up in front of Andy's apartment house. Daniel stepped out, striding around the car, and gallantly opened the door for Andy. Just as she was about to thank him, and bid her good-byes outside, she spotted Jake walking alone up the block. Impulsively she turned to Daniel.

"How about a nightcap before you head back to your hotel?"

Daniel, fully expecting a polite brush-off, was taken aback by Andy's sudden interest. Maybe the night wasn't going to be a total loss after all.

Andy was certain that Jake saw her and Daniel walk together into the building. To bring home the

101

point, she even slipped her arm through Daniel's talking animatedly all the way into her apartment.

Andy, still chatting amiably as she went in search of a rarely used bottle of cognac in one of her kitchen cabinets, flicked on the stereo as she returned, intentionally turning up the volume.

"Nice music," Daniel commented. "But I don't think we need to blast it." When Daniel walked over to lower the volume, he also switched off the overhead light. The room was imbued with a soft glow from the lamp on the end table and the dim light from the kitchen. Andy had been so preoccupied with getting back at Jake that she had totally overlooked the message Daniel was obviously reading in her behavior. She merely wanted to keep him there long enough to set Jake's imagination in motion, and then she planned to cordially send her date on his way. A pleasant chat over a brandy was definitely all she had in mind. It was not all Daniel had on his mind.

As Andy offered Daniel his drink, he took it out of her hand, setting it on the table. His other hand swept around her waist.

"Let's dance, first," he whispered seductively.

"No thanks," Andy insisted, sidestepping him. "I really am quite tired."

Clearly the wrong thing to say, Andy realized, spotting the enticing twinkle in Daniel's eye.

"I mean," she quickly amended, "that I think we had better have our nightcap and then you should be on your way."

"Relax. It's barely eleven. Or do you turn into a

pumpkin by midnight?" He kept his hands lightly on her shoulders as he gazed languidly into her eyes.

Andy was regretting by the minute what she now conceded was a childish plan. She was definitely not in the mood for fending off a persistent admirer. And from the determined gleam in his eyes, Daniel did not appear to be the kind of man who easily took no for an answer.

Retrieving his drink from the table, she once again handed it to him.

"Really, Daniel, I have to be up at the crack of dawn tomorrow morning."

When he gave her a suspicious look, she quickly explained, "I jog eight to ten miles every morning. I'm training for the marathon."

"Hey, I'm impressed," Daniel said, sipping his drink. His cornflower-blue eyes swept over her body with appreciation as well as speculation. Then, taking her hand, he led her over to the couch.

"Come sit down and tell me more about it. Jogging is one sport I've never really been able to relate to. Now tennis and racketball—those are my obsessions. Somehow running, especially all those miles, seems painfully tedious. But you must get something out of it."

Keeping a respectable distance from him on the sofa, Andy said a little irritably, "I guess you have to experience what it's like to understand the kind of feeling running gives you."

"How about if we try it out tomorrow morning?" Andy did not miss the implication that his idea was to first spend the night with her. She was becoming a little weary of the whole game.

Tiredly, she said, "I don't advise getting indoctrinated to jogging with an eight-mile run."

"How do you suggest indoctrinating me?" he murmured, his fingers toying with some strands of her hair.

Cocking her head to one side, she threw him a disparaging grimace.

Daniel laughed. "Okay, that was a lousy line. I'm usually better at this. You have me floundering here."

Andy laughed back.

"You're a very intriguing woman," Daniel whispered as he rapidly switched gears, edging closer to her. "I'm very attracted to you," he muttered breathily into her ear.

Before Andy could respond, Daniel swept his arms around her in one swift movement, pulling her fiercely to him. His lips made straight for their target. At first stunned by the suddenness of Daniel's fast move, she merely let herself be drawn against him. Quickly coming to her senses, she struggled out from his grasp, while at the same moment he was attempting to press her down on the couch. In the process one of them accidentally knocked the lamp over. It crashed loudly to the floor. Startled, Daniel, still with his arms around Andy, rolled over on the narrow couch landing on top of her on the carpet.

They both began to laugh and apologize at the same time—Andy for misleading Daniel, and Daniel for coming on with such a heavy-handed approach.

He was still half on top of her, trying to get up and help her up as well, when the front door swung open.

"What a cozy little picture," Jake said, stepping casually into the room. Andy and Daniel looked up with shocked expressions. Quickly, Daniel switched his gaze, now questioning, to Andy. Andy did not take her eyes off Jake.

"How the hell did you get in?" Andy exclaimed. She had definitely locked her door. No one forgot to do that in the city.

For an answer Jake dangled a key in his hand.

"Where did you get that?" Andy's voice reflected more amazement than anger.

"You offered it to me—when we came back from the gym this morning. Remember?"

She had handed him the extra loose key she always carried in her duffel bag, but only for him to open the door for her, paying no attention to the fact that he had omitted returning it. There were other more important things on her mind at the time.

"Get out, Jake," Andy hissed. "And leave my key behind."

"I heard something crash and thought you might be having some trouble," he said idly, making no attempt to exit.

"Well," Andy sassed, letting Daniel help her stand, "I'm perfectly fine, as you can obviously see. So please go."

Jake's expression was rigidly harsh, his smile grim as he watched Andy readjust her skirt. He remained where he was, narrowed eyes focused on her, looking like he was about to say something. But then he merely crossed his arms in front of his chest.

It was no more than a few moments—three figures frozen in motion—but it felt like an eternity to Andy, her insides churning violently. Daniel broke the spell.

"The lady asked you to leave, buddy," Daniel said, a hint of menace in his husky voice.

Jake's eyes flickered over to the large man across the room. There was a bland expression on his face, but Andy spotted that half-moon scar suddenly start to twitch. Then he switched his gaze to Andy, his thumb rubbing his chin contemplatively as he studied her.

"I always have to keep reminding myself what a fierce little competitor you are." They were almost the same words he had uttered this afternoon while they were making love. Now both the tone and meaning were harshly different. Andy flinched at the hard-edged glint in his eyes.

Then remembering that it was Jake, not her, who was the guilty party in this little scenario, she bristled. "I think those attributes are definitely misplaced. I'm not the one who will stoop to any level to get what I want," she said acidly. "So if anyone gets the award for dirty, underhanded competition, pin it on your own lapel."

Daniel, who up to now stood quietly off to the side trying to figure out what exactly was going on, took a step toward Jake.

"Maybe you and Andrea ought to discuss this

106

some other time." Daniel's words were spoken with clear warning.

"I don't have anything to discuss," Andy announced determinedly to Daniel, never taking her hostile eyes off Jake.

She could see the rage brewing behind Jake's steady gaze. And then in two strides he stalked over to her, grabbing hold of her wrist. His fingers felt like steel bands.

"You had to get back at me, didn't you?" His eyes left her face, insinuatingly traveling down her body.

"Jake, let go of me."

"And were you going to sleep with him too—just to prove a point?" he snarled, his eyes returning to stare coldly into hers as she tried to squirm free.

"I think that's enough," Daniel said hotly.

"I couldn't agree more," Jake confirmed. His expression was enigmatic as he looked intently at Andy's hand before letting go. Still he made no move to leave.

Andy felt a stab of raw pain as she looked into his eyes. Their afternoon had promised so much, and now everything was shattering around them. Even her anger didn't shroud her despair.

"You're a bastard, Jake," she muttered with more sorrow than bitterness.

Daniel, determined to take some action, bounded over to the door, opening it. "This is the way out, buddy. Unless you care to taste my fist." He clenched his hands at his sides.

"Why you . . ." Not bothering to finish his sentence, Jake swung around from Andy with a fighting look in his eye.

"Jake, this is ridiculous. Will you please stop," she implored, trying to grab hold of his shirt sleeve. He shrugged her off angrily and strode toward the door.

Unfortunately, he forgot about the coffee table that stood in his path. The wicker basket table was edged in metal, and when Jake blindly crashed into it, he bent over with a groan, clutching his knee. He eased himself onto the couch, cursing under his breath.

"Oh God, Jake, are you all right?" Andy cried as she hurried to him.

"Sure," he muttered, his face etched in a sharp scowl, "if being crippled for life doesn't bother you."

Daniel watched in confusion as she bent over Jake with clear concern.

"Hey," he snapped. "I thought you wanted to get rid of this pest."

"That doesn't mean I want to see him maimed," Andy retorted, feeling angry suddenly at both of them.

"I think you had better leave, Daniel. Now," she added for emphasis as she turned to face him. "Thanks for the dinner," she said in polite but final dismissal. A flicker of a smile parted Jake's lips.

"I'm going. Believe me, I don't need this—any of it," he quipped sarcastically, grabbing his London Fog trench coat, swinging it over one shoulder for dramatic emphasis. The front door already opened for an easy exit, Daniel walked out, slamming it angrily after him.

Alone with Jake, Andy felt suddenly awkward. "Is your knee badly hurt? Let me have a look."

Jake didn't say anything, but he grabbed her wrist when she tried to pull up his pants to see the damage.

"Leave it," he said dryly, his eyes flickering over her assessingly. In her kneeling position, she realized Jake had a perfect view down the front of her dress. Quickly standing up, she freed herself from Jake's hold.

"I'll go get you an ice pack," she said with stern determination. She could feel his eyes on her as she walked into the kitchen.

CHAPTER SEVEN

Her hands trembled as she put together a makeshift ice pack with a few ice cubes wrapped in a cotton dish towel. Within minutes she returned with it to the living room. Jake was sitting exactly where she had left him.

"I don't intend to feel any guilt about ruining your legs for running. So roll up your slacks if you don't want me to do it," she ordered matter-of-factly. Her shakiness under control, Andy was once again ready for the fight.

Jake studied her for a moment. Again she couldn't figure out what he was thinking or feeling. Then she remembered what a consummate actor he was. The memory fueled her anger even more. She chose to ignore the pain it stoked as well.

"So?" she demanded impatiently. "Are you going to cooperate?"

Silently, Jake bent over and pulled his trouser leg over the injured knee.

"It's starting to swell," she observed, annoyed that a twinge of concern came across in her voice.

"Did you think I was faking it for sympathy, nurse?" he quipped sarcastically, jerking slightly as she laid the ice pack less than gently over his knee.

"Take it easy," he snapped. "I'm going to have to give you some lessons if you intend to play Florence Nightingale."

"You've taught me all the lessons I care to learn," Andy countered.

"I'm beginning to realize that you could teach me a few as well."

"What's that supposed to mean?" she asked suspiciously. She was sitting on the edge of the wicker basket, careful not to lean provocatively forward as she tended to Jake's knee.

"Just how many men could you handle in one day?"

"How dare you?" she gasped, her hand smacking against his cheek at the same moment.

The imprint of her fingers stretched across the side of his face. She put her hand up to her mouth, wide-eyed with a mixture of rage and surprise. Her swing had been a pure reflex action.

"I shouldn't have lowered myself," she said bitingly.

"I thought you were pretty adept at lowering yourself," he retorted, rubbing his cheek.

"You are not going to be able to force my hand

111

again, Jake. I'm not the villain in this piece." She got up and walked over to the front door.

"You had better hobble on home now," she said coldly. She felt drained, a sudden feeling of weakness overcoming her.

"You're a hard woman, Andrea." He had never used her given name before, and it sounded strangely alien on his lips. He put aside the ice, slowly pulling his trouser leg down. "All this because I had a business affair to attend to." He shook his head from side to side in disappointment.

"Affair is an apt word," she said acidly as Jake walked over to where she stood at the door.

"You have quite a ways to go in learning the meaning of the word trust." The same pain and anger she felt she saw reflected in his eyes. He quietly walked out.

"I'm not the only one who needs to learn about trust." Andy's words fell against the closed door. She wondered if he heard her.

Leaning her back against the door, she could feel the cold metal penetrate through the thin silk to her skin. It didn't matter. Her insides already felt like ice.

The lamp base had shattered when it fell. Andy walked stiffly into the kitchen for the dustpan and brush. Feeling like something akin to a robot, she set about gathering the jagged pieces of pottery, sweeping them up in slow, mechanical motions. Like the pieces of her heart, she thought, and then laughed dryly at the melodramatic image. The laugh quickly

112

faded. After all it was the truth. Her heart did feel broken.

What distressed her almost as much as Jake's lack of fidelity was his biting rage. Even if it had been justified, which it wasn't, his anger felt all-encompassing in its fierceness. His acid tongue could painfully lash out. It was a side of Jake she hadn't ever seen before. Well, she thought with asperity, maybe a man scorned feels and behaves no differently than a woman scorned. And justified or not, Jake did believe that she was merrily playing the same dishonest game as he was. She had been caught in what appeared to be a very compromising position when he walked in. If it all didn't hurt so much, it might have been funny.

Switching off the stereo, she walked into her bedroom. More scattered pieces of her moments of abandon with Jake: the leftover remnants of a barely eaten lunch tossed on the tray on the end table; her velour jogging suit lying in a heap on the floor where she had flung it in her wanton strip; the unmade bed, its crumpled sheets attesting to the passion of their lovemaking. Her eyes filled with pain as she walked over to the edge of the bed. Bending down, she picked up her running outfit, her hands stroking the velvety softness, trying to feel some comfort. There was none.

Reaching her hand behind her back, she unzipped her dress, shrugging it off her shoulders, and let it fall silently to the floor. She stepped out of it and continued to undress. As she started to reach for her nightgown in her bureau drawer, Andy caught a

113

reflection of herself in the mirror. The image held her fixed. The longer and harder she looked, the angrier she became. Drawing in a deep breath, her rage mounted at the realization that Jake had somehow successfully switched the tables on her. She was the one walking around feeling miserable. Jake had skipped merrily out laying this guilt trip on her for behaving disreputably. Damn him, she fumed, he was the one that had left her in a blasé fashion to go frolicking with the more-than-willing Janine Rossetti.

Doing an abrupt about-face, Andy stormed back over to the bed and threw on her jogging suit. So he thought he was going to get the last word, did he?

She was so absorbed in her litany of charges that she almost walked right by his door. She waited tensely after ringing the doorbell twice. Her nerves almost got the better of her as she heard Jake's footsteps approaching the door.

All the time Jake had lived here, Andy had intentionally avoided his apartment. At first it had been a response caused by her anger at his moving onto her home turf. Later, she found herself staying clear because of her own fears of becoming too intimate.

Jake opened the door, a warm light flowing out of the apartment and bathing him in its soft glow. He looked so uncompromising standing there staring formidably at her. But Andy refused to be intimidated. It wasn't easy, especially as she found it hard to look into his cold eyes and harder still to avoid straying to his broad expanse of chest, now bare. The memory of how his firm, muscled body had felt pressed against her naked flesh almost made her turn around and bolt back up to her apartment.

Willing herself to regain her composure, she said defiantly, "I don't think we've finished our conversation." With a wry smile, she amended, "At least I haven't."

When he made no move to step aside, her voice showed a little more discomfort.

"May I come inside to talk?"

He gestured her to enter, standing back so that she could step into the entry hall.

"Thanks." She hoped her voice displayed more control than she felt inside of her.

They stood silently staring at each other for a few moments, Jake still not having spoken. Finally he said dryly, "If you have a lot to say, we might as well go into the living room and sit down."

Limping slightly, he led the way to a room about the same size as Andy's. There was no bay window, but there was a fireplace. Though different than her own, this one was equally beautiful. Finely crafted of an ebony marble surrounded by an intricately carved mantel painted white, it was the focal point of the room, its stark contrast of light and dark mirrored in the carpet and furnishings. A charcoal-gray sectional sofa rested on a soft creamy-white carpet, and even the paintings on the wall were a striking blend of light and dark hues. The room exuded a very masculine aura. Andy had to remind herself she hadn't come here tonight to study interior design.

The sectional sofa made deciding where to sit awkward. Andy would have preferred a separate chair, thus insuring the distance she found herself wanting desperately. Feeling brittle and uneasy, she sat down on a corner section of the couch.

"Drink?" His tone was impersonally polite.

Andy shook her head from side to side. A drink was the last thing she needed. She felt uncomfortably light-headed enough right now.

Jake, favoring his injured leg, walked to a cabinet near the large double window and brought out a bottle of Scotch. Taking it neat, he returned with his half-finished drink to the couch. Sitting with nonchalant ease two cushions away from Andy, he lifted his legs and stretched his arms out, resting them comfortably on the back of the sofa. He continued to hold his drink, but made no movement to have any more of it.

Doggedly, Andy began. "You had no right to jump to such tacky, insulting conclusions tonight. Daniel Reed was nothing more than a charming, entertaining dinner date."

"I noticed how entertaining he was. Quite talented, obviously." Jake snickered.

Andy could feel herself reddening. "There you go again. Maybe it's just the unfortunate product of a dirty mind. You may find it perfectly easy to have a multitude of affairs going at the same time, but I don't."

"My, my. So now it's multitudes, is it," he said tauntingly.

Flushing, Andy snapped, "Well who knows how many women you manage to keep happy." Tit for tat, she smiled tightly, disappointed to see that the

116

red marks from her slap had vanished from his cheek. She found herself wishing it could have been a more lasting reminder of her outrage.

"Well, as difficult as it may be for you to believe, and as much as my manhood hates to admit it, I only saw Janine tonight. We had such a delightful time together that I opted to cancel my other rendezvous. The rest of the harem will have to wait until the morning."

"Poor things." She sighed deprecatingly. They had both gotten caught up in this adolescent game, and Andy, wanting to stop it, didn't know how.

Reaching for some semblance of maturity, she finally said, "Can't we hash this out like two adults?"

"What is there to hash out?" he asked grimly. "Not only did you immediately assume that my meeting with Janine was personal, you were willing to pay me back for my supposed crime by jumping in the sack with someone else for spite. I don't find either of those responses particularly admirable."

"And just how admirable is it of you to assume my guilt?" She lifted one eyebrow questioningly.

"I walked in on you, remember?"

Andy had to admit to herself that the picture of her and Daniel interlocked on the floor did not look particularly platonic. She began to smile.

"Care to fill me in on the humor? I'm having some difficulty imagining what could be so amusing," he admonished her bitingly.

Her laugh vanished. In a steady voice, her expression serious, she said, "What you witnessed was not the beginning of a love scene. Daniel had made an advance, but I was not reciprocating. In our brief little struggle, we knocked over the lamp and fell onto the floor. He was in the process of apologizing when you barged in." All of a sudden she looked sharply at him. "Just why did you barge in like that?"

Now it was Jake's turn to flush. "I told you," he faltered, "I heard the commotion as I passed your door, and I thought you might have been having some trouble. That creep could have been trying to rape you, for all I knew."

A little smile curled the edges of her lips. "For a while there I thought I was in the middle of a grade B melodrama. No—on second thought, more a grade B slapstick comedy."

"You did, did you?" Jake snarled, but there was a teasing hint of a smile on his lips. Andy's explanation about her and Daniel had begun to soften his features. "You have a very warped sense of humor if you think a busted kneecap is funny."

"Well, no one asked you to come on like Mr. Macho, and then go storming across the room to try to take a punch at the poor guy."

"Poor guy! That ape probably eats small children and women for breakfast."

"You're the one that looked like you could have devoured a few innocent people—with me for your entrée." She flashed him a quick grin.

"You're right," he said softly, his gaze intense. "And as angry as I am at your childish game, I'm still hungry for you."

"No, Jake. Don't." He had closed the distance

118

between them, his hands reaching for her. Her look was pleading. But when he drew her against him, her cheek pressing against his warm flesh, she was flooded with intimate remembrances. Andy stayed put for a moment, but as Jake's arms encircled her more passionately, she pushed him away.

"Jake, please," Andy beseeched.

"Please what? Please stop, or please don't stop?" Jake taunted, a glimmer of a smile on his lips.

"You are all wrong about me," she said softly. "I'm a one-man woman. It was unfair of me to use Daniel to try to make you jealous. It was childish and—pointless. I would never have slept with him. He didn't interest me in the least. You're the only man on my mind." She sighed deeply, looking at him with sad eyes. "We just see things so differently." She stood up, walking over to the mantel. Fingering a lovely ceramic bird sculpture on the shelf, she turned back to Jake.

"Remember that first time we—we kissed? At the track?" she added, to make sure he remembered.

He needed no reminders. The feel of her lips never left his memory after that day. Jake nodded, a softness infusing his features.

"You accused me of being afraid every man I met wanted nothing more than to get me in bed and then abandon me."

"Andy, I . . ."

"No, Jake, let me finish." She gently lifted her fingers from the delicate bird. "It was an overstatement." She paused for only a moment. "But there was some truth to your words." She walked back to the couch and sat down beside him.

What she wanted to say wasn't easy. Clearing her throat, she forced herself to go on. "I'm generally very cautious and clearheaded when it comes to men. Usually I have this sixth sense that seems to rally forth at crucial moments. Like radar, a warning beep goes off, and suddenly the guy comes into clear focus. Frequently not a flattering picture, but it has saved me from making some unfortunate mistakes."

Jake turned toward her on the couch, quiet but acutely attentive.

"A few years ago my radar must have gone haywire. I got involved in a relationship with a man at work. The classic story, really." Andy laughed deprecatingly. "Naïve young woman falls madly in love with older, sophisticated boss, who just happens to be married. Miserably, of course, with vows that he is separated and promises of an imminent divorce —that always seems to be waiting for the right moment. Which never comes along." Andy fell silent. It still hurt to realize how guileless she had been.

"I know about your relationship with Ken Haggerty," Jake said gently.

"Do you? I'm not surprised. There are still a couple of people at the office who seem to take pleasure in maintaining an image of me as a ruthless career climber who would think nothing of sleeping with a supervisor if it meant a promotion." She was thinking particularly of Sandra Kennedy, her staff member who could not only be lazy on any number of occasions but be catty as well. Andy had had a meet-

120

ing with her this week where she had made it clear to Sandra that if she didn't show more attention to her work, she'd have to start looking for another job.

Andy had noticed Sandra eyeing Jake with more than casual interest on numerous occasions. She would not have been at all surprised if Sandra had been the one to confide in Jake her version of Andy's affair with Ken.

"That was the implication," Jake confirmed.

"It's funny. In some ways I almost prefer that rendition. At least then I wouldn't have to feel so painfully foolish and gullible for believing Ken really wanted to marry me."

Jake reached out to her, and lifting her downcast chin up to face him, he said gently, "I prefer your version. In fact I never doubted it. You play hard at work, but I don't believe you play dirty. I'm sorry you had to go through all that suffering. But I can't honestly say I'm sorry it didn't work out the way you wanted. We wouldn't be here right now."

"That leads me to my next point," Andy said, the edge returning to her voice as she removed Jake's hand from her face. "It's happening again."

Jake eyed her with a puzzled expression.

"My sixth sense—my radar," she clarified. "It was functioning beautifully until you came along. Oh, a few little bleeps crossed the screen, but I ignored them. I wanted you so much." She took in a little gasp of air. "But the simple truth is, I do not go in for casual sex. I believe in all the old virtues—love, honor, fidelity." She emphasized the last. "I can't take our relationship lightly, Jake, and I'd rather not

121

take it at all," she finished softly, the words almost melting into the air.

"You forgot another one of the tried and true virtues," Jake chided gently.

"Which one is that?"

"Trust." He smiled wistfully. "I guess we both overlooked that one at varying moments today."

"Let's not start that again. Look, we have to face it. It's the old double standard. You can be filled with irate jealousy at the thought that I would cheat on you, but I just don't believe you have any qualms about indulging in some extra fun and games with a sexy and obliging bombshell." Thinking about Janine again started Andy's blood boiling.

"Janine was at her luscious best tonight," Jake acknowledged blithely, an unabashed smile on his lips.

Andy was outraged at his total lack of concern for her feelings. She shot up from the couch to get away from him. He caught hold of her, sending her tumbling back down. In the process she fell against his injured knee.

Grimacing with pain, he commanded, "Careful of my knee, you little hellion."

"You bastard," she sputtered. "You're enjoying all of this, aren't you?"

Jake leaned half over her, his hands firmly pinning down her shoulders. She was helplessly restrained.

"As I was saying before you so rudely interrupted"—Jake sighed with practiced nonchalance—"Janine was a delightful hostess—warm, alluring, and captivating."

122

Andy lowered her lids, turning her head to the side in an effort to tune him out.

"Her husband couldn't get enough of her all during dinner."

Andy's eyes shot open as she lifted her head to gape at Jake.

"Charming, attractive fellow—obviously infatuated with his wife. It made it a bit difficult discussing business with the two of them." He studied her critically as he finished.

"Her husband?" Andy whispered tentatively.

"Now don't start suggesting I go in for ménage à trois," he accused mockingly. "I always prefer one-on-one relationships." He was deliberately taunting her.

All of a sudden the whole picture came into focus. Green eyes flashing as the light dawned, she declared acidly, "You knew all along. The whole time I was suffering those awful pangs of jealousy, you knew Janine was married—that her husband would be there. You intentionally let me believe it was going to be the two of you alone together." A cold anger stabbed her, heightening even more as he nodded in agreement. "You really are hateful."

"I didn't actually plan to lead you on, Andy. It was you who started it. You were so immediately suspicious, so automatically distrusting. Here I had just made passionate love to you, and within minutes you were conjuring up fantasies of my next conquest." Now it was Jake's turn to get mad. "What the hell kind of a guy do you think I am? I thought you understood me better than that."

123

Andy felt as though she'd just been landed a blow to her gut. He was right. She had quickly and easily jumped to her own conclusions. It had seemed so obvious at the time. But now she clearly saw that she had given Jake no credit for being a man of honesty and integrity.

"I wanted to teach you a lesson in trust." Jake's voice was harsh, but his features reflected sadness.

A mixture of shame, anger, and relief brewed inside of her. As badly as she felt for misjudging him, she thought his lesson needlessly hurtful. But she could not deny her happiness in learning that Jake had not sauntered off to bed with another woman.

"I get your point, Jake. But I also think if this relationship is going to have any chance at all then we both have to be more straightforward and honest with one another. We're too old to be playing such adolescent games."

"You're right. Honesty is the best policy." Jake grinned, sliding down on his good knee in front of her, his hands pressed sensuously on her upper thighs. Warm brown eyes sparkled as he looked up at her. "Can I tell you something honest right now?" His voice was a husky whisper.

A captivating flush rose on Andy's cheeks, the caressing quality of his voice fast cutting though her hard-fought composure.

"What's that?" she murmured, unable to shift her eyes from his penetrating gaze.

"I want to kiss and make up." His hands gently stroked her thighs, slowly traveling upward until he reached her waist, his fingers slipping slightly under

124

the elastic band. The feel of his touch against her skin was electrifying.

"I think this is going to become my favorite outfit to watch you get out of." He grinned, his voice softly seductive.

"And just what makes you think I plan to take it off again?" She couldn't resist teasing him a little, even though his magical touch had already begun to madden her with desire and she, too, longed to make up.

"What makes me think that?" His fingers skimmed across her mouth. "Maybe it's your lips, half-parted and inviting me to taste them and the many wonders that lie within," he whispered, planting a butterfly kiss on each corner of her lips. Then he pressed his head against her breast. "Or maybe it's the erratic, frantic pounding of your heart. I can hear it beating, 'Take me, take me.' " He looked up into her twinkling eyes. "Shall I continue to point out the parts of you that tell me you want me desperately." His hand slipped beneath the waistband of her pants.

"You've convinced me," she said breathlessly, reaching for the top snap of her jacket.

Jake drew her hand away. "Here, let me have a turn." His nimble fingers easily undid the snaps in rapid succession, his lips hungry to taste her sweet, succulent nipples. The deep rosy-hued buds had already begun to peak, but Jake's mouth fully awakened them, his tongue circling in erotic, tantalizing swirls.

Hungrily, Andy locked her arms around his neck, pressing Jake's lips more tightly to her breast, her back arched in passionate yearning. This was what she longed for, what she had despairingly feared she had lost. God, don't let us fight again, she entreated the heavens. I love him so. I don't think I could bear not belonging to him body and soul.

She cried out in pleasure as Jake's tongue very lightly began to sweep tender brushstrokes across her breasts and down to her firm, flat stomach. His hands tugged her pants down just far enough to expose her perfectly formed navel. His tongue now teased and tantalized this utterly sensitive spot, driving Andy to a fever pitch.

Fiercely she began kneading Jake's shoulders, sliding her knuckles down the center of his back and up again. She slid down the couch to caress him further. Jake's sharp cry, clearly pain not desire, made her leap back up onto the couch.

"Oh, darling, I'm sorry. Your knee—I forgot."

"So did I." He grinned reassuringly. "This is going to take some clever figuring out."

"Maybe we ought to wait," she offered, her voice etched with a disappointment she could not disguise. Her body still trembled with a fiery need, but it was tempered by her real concern for Jake.

"Am I to take that to mean you are devoid of innovative ideas?" he asked with a teasing grin.

"Is that a challenge?" she countered.

"If you care to take it on," he murmured, his hands idly stroking the velour cloth between her thighs.

"Actually, I'd rather take it off," she laughed

throatily, standing so that she slipped between his parted thighs. "Care to help?"

"I always like to be helpful." He caught hold of her pants at her ankles. Slowly tugging, his eyes on line with her navel, he gradually pulled them down. His tongue marked each spot on her soft, warm flesh that was freed from the covering. Andy would never know by what miracle she was able to maintain her stance during his erotic foray. Her legs felt like rubber, melting with the heat of his blandishments.

When at last Jake slipped the unwanted pants over her ankles and tossed them aside, he stood up beside her.

"What now?" he teased as they stood face to face, his hands lightly resting on her hips.

"Oh, I might be able to come up with a creative idea or two." She grabbed hold of the front of his pants. Jake caught his breath as she undid the closure in one smooth, swift movement. The palms of her hands skimmed his bare flesh from waist to thigh as she eased his pants down to his knees. Then dropping to a kneeling position, she gently, carefully eased the material over his injured knee and finally off him completely. With infinite tenderness she pressed her lips against the bruise, becoming less cautious as her mouth traveled up his thigh.

When she stood before him again, Jake slipped his hand down the gentle curve of her back to her buttocks and pressed her soft yielding body against his.

"Are you game?" Andy whispered her question in his ear, her tongue punctuating her words.

"Baby, I have no idea what you're cooking in that

127

torrid little mind of yours, but right now I am game for anything on your mind." He laughed wickedly.

Guessing the right door, Andy found the bathroom. Jake in tow, she walked over to the shower. Turning on the faucet, she swung back to Jake. "Warm water is very soothing to injuries, don't you agree?"

"I'd say it was just what the doctor ordered."

They stepped into the small enclosure, their bodies pressed together out of longing as well as lack of space. As the water pulsated over them, they began to embrace. Their kisses became hungrier and greedier as their longing heightened. Suddenly, as though the falling water had made her weightless, Jake easily lifted her up in his arms, her back pressed up against the wall of the shower. Swinging her long limbs around his thighs, she moaned her need, her lips finding his and plying him with urgent kisses, her hands stroking his back and arms.

Clinging to him now, arms locked around his neck, her ankles crossed behind his back, she gasped as he guided her down onto him. A sharp cry of exquisite pleasure escaped her throat as he made the first thrust and she experienced once more the ecstasy of their union.

"I love you." The words rolled off her lips as he led her to the peak of pleasure. And when Jake whispered back "Oh, baby, I love you, too," tears—sweet, warm tears of joy—tumbled down her cheeks.

CHAPTER EIGHT

"Please, Jake," Andy entreated, turning her collar up against the biting January chill. "Let's not start that one again."

Jake grabbed her elbow, his fingers penetrating through her down parka, pulling her to a halt. "How long do you intend to keep our little secret?" His cool sarcasm was not meant to be missed as he flung the question at her. "I didn't know I was going to be doomed to stay a closet lover forever."

"Don't go melodramatic on me again." Andy sighed, trying to tug free to no avail.

Jake's features softened, but he still held her firm. "Andy, would you please tell me what the big deal is about meeting for lunch? I give you my solemn oath I won't seduce you under the table."

Andy looked at him with an expression that said he knew damn well that wasn't the issue. Still, once again she went through her little speech. "It's not just getting together for lunch once or twice. It's regularly going out alone together every time you're working inside. Plus, walking to work together and walking back home together; even picking me up last week in my bug. That was really clever. It was lucky only Larry and Paula from my own department saw you. They aren't the types to go blabbing around that we're an item." She shrugged her shoulders in exasperation. "You may not think much of company policy, Jake. But I have no intention of giving Foster any ammunition to use on me again. I warned you over two months ago when we started this—this relationship that I would not have anyone at work know what's going on in our private lives. And you promised"—she emphasized her words with a poke at his chest—"that you would respect my wishes."

"Then how about a secret rendezvous in the boiler room? You could claim a sudden desire to stoke the fire, and I could sneak down and help you." He leaned over to kiss her, catching her cheek as she turned her head away. "Mmmm, woman—I definitely think your fires need some stoking."

"You are impossible." She laughed, her frustration at his blatant display of affection taking a backseat. He always managed to seduce her out of her annoyance, with either his words or his actions.

She loved him, and she wished their relationship could be more open. Being surreptitious wasn't exactly her choice either. But she kept her thoughts to herself, knowing that if Jake got even an inkling that

130

she might be weakening he would move right in to get his way.

"That's it," he announced, slipping his hand in hers as they started walking again. "Today's the day. I'm going to stomp into that old buzzard's office and have it out with him. Nobody governs Jake Downing's choice of playmates, and just because old Foster happens to employ one of the most luscious, delectable numbers this side of Chicago does not mean that I can't play with her."

"Playmate? Luscious number? My, aren't we macho this morning," she said with enough sarcastic bite for Jake to look momentarily contrite.

"I must have eaten too much bacon this morning. Generally I stay away from chauvinist pigs." He grinned. "I promise not to demean you in front of Foster. How about if I simply call you the love of my life? Now how could he keep two desperate lovers apart?"

For a sinking moment Andy took him seriously. All she needed was for Jake to confront Foster about his staunch policy. She could almost physically feel herself being unceremoniously propelled out the door. Good-bye career. Luckily, she quickly spied the twinkle in his eyes as he ambled down the street whistling a lilting tune.

"Has anyone ever told you that you are a character?" she asked affectionately.

"You mean besides my folks, my sisters, my teachers, my dates and their parents—why, no. Oh, wait, my father always told me I was a nut. Does that count?"

He quickly pinched her bottom.

"Jake!"

"It's okay, it's okay. The coast was clear. I checked before I squeezed."

Andy tried to regain her composure as they turned the corner to the office. She knew that several people at work were beginning to surmise that something was going on between her and Jake, but she was determined to give no one anything concrete for evidence. It was not easy, given Jake's wily ways.

"Don't forget," he whispered breathily in her ear as he opened the door for her, "three o'clock in the boiler room."

"You'll have to stoke that fire alone," she said tartly, keeping her expression perfectly bland, and then she hurried ahead of him, having spotted Sandra Kennedy at the bottom of the stairs.

Sandra smiled in what Andy knew was forced politeness. She had no doubt that Sandra was boiling inside now that Andy had insisted on personally checking all of her protocols. Too many mistakes had gone out to clients that came directly from Sandra's desk. What irked Andy was that Sandra couldn't seem to appreciate how far she was going to keep from having to fire her. With the economy the way it was, and the unemployment rate escalating by the hour, Andy didn't have the heart to force anyone out of a job. But even she could be pushed only so far.

Stopping at her secretary's desk for a few minutes, she gathered up the mail, her messages, and the current protocols and listened with affectionate amusement to the latest saga of her secretary Sheila's persistent quest for wealth and love, in that order.

"The loser didn't even own a car. And then he has the nerve to suggest we take the MBTA back to my apartment. Not even a taxi! Can you beat that?" her secretary groaned. "And the guy was dressed to the nines, straight out of Louis' Men's Shop, so you know it had to really cost." Only twenty-three, small, blond, and pertly pretty, Sheila shook her perfectly coiffed shoulder-length hair from side to side. "And after taking out this unbelievable wad of bills to pay for my drinks, and acting like a suave, supersophisticated dude, he tells me that he's in some damn computer programming school."

"Well, you know the old saying, Sheila, my girl. You can't tell a book by its cover." As Sheila groaned anew, Andy laughed. "Why not use a more direct approach when you're scouting around your next singles bar. Ask the guy to show you his financial statement first: bank account, investment portfolio, what page of *Who's Who* he's on."

"You may act snide, Andrea Howard, but my mother always told me, 'Sheila, my sweetheart, it's as easy to love a rich man as a poor one.'" She nodded her head up and down for final emphasis.

"I suppose mama knows best." Andy chuckled, sorting through her mail as she walked toward her office. As she got to the door, she turned back to face Sheila. "Just remember, Sheila, sweetheart, to check the guy's wedding ring finger for a white band, and if that checks out, make sure to ask him what his alimony payments cost him a month."

"I don't know how someone could be only twenty-eight years old and already so cynical. You could use some good, old-fashioned lover to warm the cockles of your cold, cold heart." Sheila winked, confirming what Andy had already guessed. God, did everyone in the place know she was involved with Jake?

Sheila smiled, her look clearly saying, "Don't worry, your secret is safe with me."

Andy didn't doubt it. Sheila had immediately assigned Andy the role of big sister soon after she became Andy's secretary. She had confided enough in Andy to seal the bonds of trust forever. Andy smiled back, switching the topic to business at hand.

"I have a ten o'clock meeting with the staff, so be sure to get the Dempsey material together for me about a half hour before they all stampede in here."

"I already started getting it in order," Sheila assured her.

"Great."

Andy settled down behind her desk, taking care of the mail first and next her stack of pink message slips. Finally she began to tackle the stack of protocols on her desk, purposely placing Sandra's work on the bottom of the pile. She decided that she didn't need to get aggravated first thing Monday morning. And inevitably Sandra managed to do something to cause her grief. Not enough to warrant being called on the carpet, but just enough to be annoying. She made a mental note to give Sandra another month, and then she would at least see about getting her transferred to a less demanding department. Happy with her guilt-free decision, she soon became engrossed in the rest of her work.

The group filed out of her office. Larry, the last to leave, turned to her at the door. Andy once again gave him a reassuring nod and a smile of confidence. As soon as the door closed, leaving her alone at last, the dauntless, self-assured pose crumbled.

It was only rumor, Andy tried in vain to remind herself. She hadn't heard a word from downstairs. Surely Ted would have discussed something so drastic with her first and foremost. After all, she would be the most greatly affected by it.

"Oh, Jake, let me get my hands on you," she hissed out loud. "If you pulled this stunt, I am going to declare all-out war." She felt better for having vowed her pledge, regardless of the fact that the man himself was not there to hear it.

"Lunch?"

Andy's eyes shot over to the door.

"Well, speak of the devil," she muttered threateningly.

"So you haven't been able to get me off your mind all morning," he quipped, disregarding her biting words and even more biting look. As he perched himself on the corner of her desk next to her chair, he skimmed the back of his hand down her cheek. Not stopping, he slid his palm down to her breast, almost cupping it before she abruptly tilted her chair as far back as it would go.

"Are you crazy? Suppose my secretary walked in

while you were sampling the merchandise?" she muttered under her breath.

"Sheila has already tripped off to lunch. I passed her skipping gaily down the hall. That girl doesn't have all her marbles, but what the hell, she's a cute little number." His hand snaked out, snatching the arm of her swivel chair. He pulled it over to him.

Sliding off the desk, he bent over her chair, both hands firmly holding either arm. "So what do you say? Do we stroll down to the boiler room, or do I ravish you right here?"

"Jake, I am not in the mood for your little seductive jests today. Especially not after my most illuminating staff meeting."

"I smell trouble." Jake continued to tease.

"Just tell me straight out. Did you or did you not go to Foster with a proposal to revamp my department?"

"The light is dawning. I'm beginning to see what is getting your sweet little—uhm, back up."

"Did you or didn't you? A simple yes or no will do. Preferably—most preferably, no."

"Yes and no."

"Run that one by me again," she said curtly, her suspicions mounting.

"Yes, I did discuss the research department's designs and formats, and no, I did not suggest a total revamping of your little nest." He leaned back against the desk, releasing his hold on her chair. "Now do I get executed, or do we fool around a little on our lunch break?"

"I'm leaning toward execution," she said, smiling coolly.

"I'm innocent, believe me. I spouted out a lot of ideas to Foster about all kinds of things, your department being a small, insignificant tack-on. The old guy didn't even comment on any of my rantings." Then becoming more serious, he said, "You know, babe, you can't always hold on to the status quo. Sometimes we can all use a little jolt—otherwise we start to stagnate, our ideas get stale, old hat."

He used "we," but Andy knew he was particularly addressing her. She resented his point of view, but there was a nagging disquiet as she tried honestly to ascertain whether the shoe he was throwing at her fit.

"I'm not saying that we all couldn't use a gentle shove if we get complacent about our work. But if you have any criticisms to make about how I run my department, I'd appreciate your making them directly to me."

"I promise, only if you promise not to bite my head off if I do point out a little weakness here or there." Jake grinned, his half-moon scar disappearing in the crease at the left-hand corner of his mouth.

Andy watched the curved arc vanish. "I think I finally figured out how you got that scar. One day you must have said a few words too many, and a woman, provoked beyond reason, maimed you for life. And if you don't watch your step, Mr. Downing, I'm going to take care of the other side of your mouth."

"Is it me or my spaghetti?" Andy had been watch-

137

ing Jake twirl the same forkful of pasta for the past two minutes. He'd been distracted all evening. In fact, ever since their confrontation two weeks ago when she had told him to keep his nose out of her department, he had seemed frequently preoccupied.

"Jake, come back to earth?" she teased.

"Sorry," Jake said gently, his face softening into a smile. "I've been running something through my head since this afternoon."

"How about running it by me?" Andy had a sudden disquieting feeling in the pit of her stomach.

Leaning toward her, elbows propped on the table, Jake peered at Andy and then regarded his plateload of food. His reluctance to begin talking was obvious. He kept moving the dish of spaghetti away from him, inch by inch.

"Please, Jake, you better tell me what's going on because I'm already beginning to imagine the worst. Is there a wife and kids back in Chicago, or are you about to take a new job in Alaska but you plan to drop me a line on occasion?" She tried for humor, but it fell flat, landing with a dull thud.

Jake cleared his throat, looking at her thoughtfully. "I've got to preface what I have to tell you."

"Uh-oh. This is going to be worse than I feared," Andy moaned, forcing a smile of encouragement onto her face.

"The thing is, I honestly believe that you are extremely bright, creative, organized, and diligent. Your staff clearly respects and admires you, and they work their butts off for you. . . ."

"Why is it your words are somehow not coming across as compliments?"

"Listen, Andy, you know that I'm sometimes brash, outspoken, determined to set things around me spinning. It's the way I work."

Her relief that Jake wasn't about to skip out on their relationship was short-lived, her anger escalating by the minute.

"You put your nose into my department, isn't that what you're telling me?"

"Remember a couple of weeks ago when you got so uptight about my casual—let me emphasize that word, casual—exchange with Foster about some new approaches in compiling the research protocols?"

Eyes narrowed and tight-lipped, Andy merely nodded.

"Foster has asked me if I would draw up a detailed proposal incorporating my ideas. He thinks it might help promote business to beef up the way we make our presentations."

Jake sat back in his chair quietly waiting for the bomb to drop. Instead, Andy sat silently for a few minutes, and then scraping back her chair, she slowly gathered up the barely touched dinner plates and carried them into the kitchen.

Staying put for a moment, Jake got up, grabbing the salt and pepper shakers, and followed her into the cramped space.

"I know you're angry, babe. I understand."

Andy flicked her eyes over him quickly and began resolutely dumping the uneaten food into the trash.

Jake removed the dish from her hand and set it in

the sink. Taking hold of her, he pinned her against the cabinets.

"Don't give me the silent treatment. Tell me what you're thinking."

She didn't fight being held fast, but she also didn't have any intention of cooperating. First of all, she was so angry that she couldn't organize her thoughts well enough to tell him how furious she felt, and secondly, if she tried to talk, she was sure she'd say things she would later regret.

"Go home, Jake" was all she would risk verbalizing.

"I am not leaving this apartment until we've talked this thing out. Honestly, I never dreamed Foster would pursue my crazy rantings."

"Obviously Foster doesn't find them crazy at all." Damn him, he was roping her into this conversation despite herself.

"Believe it or not, I have no desire to spend my free time revamping the research department. I'm a sales coordinator, and I've got enough pressures there to keep my ulcer active enough." He grinned, but Andy's face might have been carved in stone for all the response she displayed. "What do you want me to do?" He sighed, tossing his hands up in the air.

"How about quitting and finding someplace else to turn upside down with your brilliant ideas?"

Her features came alive again, rage flushing her cheeks. She shoved him away and stormed back into the living room.

Jake followed. "Can you at least try to look on the positive side of it?"

Andy threw him a look that could kill. Then, sitting down, her elbows digging into her thighs, hands propping up her chin, she muttered, "I knew this whole thing wouldn't work. For the first time I understand why Foster has always been adamant about keeping professional ties just that, purely professional. Oh, Jake, I want to come home from work eager for the arms of my true love. I want to be able to bitch and complain about all the hassles of the day, rant and rave about some bastard who's trying to step all over me." She shot him a sorrowful glance. "But what do you do when the bastard and your true love are one and the same?" Jake came over and bent down in front of her. Pulling her hands from her chin, he tugged her onto the floor next to him.

"I love you," he said softly into her ear.

"Wasn't it enough that you landed the sales coordinator job? Now you've got to take it all over?"

"Andy . . ." He put his arms around her, but she edged away.

"Hold it, Jake. There is something you had better understand. I have no intention of sitting back and letting you breeze in and reorganize everything I've worked on for years. You better plan to do battle, because I'm going to fight you tooth and nail."

"You could join me instead, you know."

"Huh?"

"We could work together on this thing. Or are you so stuck in your old ways that you can't imagine making changes?"

He was sure she'd explode, but instead she looked at him thoughtfully. "Maybe you're right. Maybe I

141

have gone along with a structure that could use some refreshing. But let me tell you, buddy"—she pointed her finger at him with a grimace—"if, after I spend some time reevaluating my department, I decide there are some areas that could be restructured, I will do it—alone. We'll both work up our ideas and individually present them to Foster, and he can make the final decision."

"That's a deal. May the best man win." Jake caught her hand in a firm shake and then proceeded to plant a row of kisses up her arm, neck, and ending at her ear, where he whispered, "Let's go to bed."

Karen munched on a cracker as she listened to her friend's tirade.

"So now Jake stalks downstairs to his desk every night, and I stalk over to mine, and we both busily try to come up with ideas that we think will top the other person. It's crazy," Andy concluded. "We're both so damned competitive. And the thing is, I know Jake really doesn't give a hoot about reorganizing my department. He did shoot off his mouth and got his foot stuck there. The only reason he's putting in all this effort is because he's as muleheaded and stubborn as I am. I offered the challenge, and he's simply lapping it up." Andy picked up a sesame breadstick and crunched into it.

As the waiter brought their chef's salads to their table, Andy looked at Karen apologetically. "Sorry for going on this whole time. Tell me something nice so I can get my mind off my woes."

Karen laughed. "You and Jake are quite a pair.

Heaven help us all if you two procreate. I can't imagine what your kids will be like with that combination of genes."

"You're not helping me, friend. The idea of marriage and a family has crossed my mind more than once over the past few months. But Jake is positively mum on the subject. The truth is we're both scared witless about making an even deeper commitment. We get into so many hassles now, it's hard to imagine what life would be like if we each didn't have our own corners to go hide in for a while until the current storm blows over."

"Marriage doesn't have to mean you're tied together in bondage," Karen said, laughing. "But I guess I'm the wrong one to talk. After seeing a guy more than a few times, I always beat a fast path away before things get too involved."

"Who are you running out on now?" Andy laughed back. "Tell me about the trials and tribulations of your love life for a while."

"Actually, I'm not running out yet. I recently met a very exciting young entrepreneur. He's an unbelievable dynamo, and he formed this little company on a shoestring. But watch out for this business because it's going to take off like a rocket in a few months. I'm even considering dropping a few bucks into the venture myself. He's coming out with a revolutionary line of computer software. Right now he's keeping a low profile, not wanting his competitors to get wind of it before he figures out the best marketing approach. Actually, I put in a good word for your company to do some marketing research for him."

143

"If it's going to be as big as you say, it would be quite a coup to land that account."

"Move in fast. He hasn't approached anyone else yet, so Horizons could easily beat out the competition."

"It would be one more big feather in Jake's cap," Andy said a little ruefully.

"Oops, I forgot," Karen said with a grin. "You two are fierce competitors."

"That's not very complimentary. I may still want him to disappear from Horizons at times, but I do love the guy. And I couldn't ever purposely deny him a terrific opportunity." She cast Karen a wicked grin. "Besides, maybe if he gets all involved in this new account, he'll forget about his precious research proposal."

"In that case I'll buzz Jim and tell him to expect a call from Jake." Karen scribbled down the information and handed it to Andy. Feeling much better, Andy set about devouring her chef's salad.

That night she told Jake the news. He was excited, especially as the computer industry was such a new and untapped source for some imaginative marketing schemes. Once he got his foot in the door, it would open the way for him to land other computer company accounts.

"How come you're being so good to me?" He pulled her down on his lap on the sofa. "My probation will be up soon, and this account, if I do land it, will insure me a permanent position."

"You told me yourself. I'm not a dirty fighter. I

144

believe in earning what I get, fair and square. Besides"—she grinned impishly, seductively unbuttoning his shirt and stroking his bare chest—"the better you do, the better the chance you'll get promoted, and I'm still next in line for your job."

"Does that mean you don't mind following in the shadow of a great man?" Jake slid his hand underneath the silky fabric of her shirt, resting it on her breast.

"Don't push your luck, babe"—Andy grinned—"or I just might start taking lessons in dirty dealing."

"I have a perfect idea. How about leading me into the bedroom, and I'll follow in your shadow tonight. That will make us even."

Andy ran her hands down Jake's long, muscled body, every curve, every ripple a part of him she knew by heart but never tired of rediscovering once more. And this evening they both seemed more relaxed, more emotionally in tune with each other than they had been in a while. The pressures of working together had begun to affect their lovemaking.

Tonight felt perfect. Lying side by side, Andy swung one slender leg over Jake's thigh, clinging to him as he hungrily kissed her, exploring the warm depths of her mouth with expert skill. Andy could feel Jake's passion growing, but she knew he would hold out, bringing her first to the same peak of desire. Her body was already trembling as Jake's lips floated down her throat, his hands lovingly stroking the wonderful curve of her body that went from the side

145

of her breast along the crook of her waist and then sleekly down her outer thigh.

Jake's exploring fingers glided over her ribs, and reaching her breasts, he gently nudged her over on her back, his palms now brushing against her ripe nipples. Arching her back, Andy made soft purring sounds, her long fingers spread against his chest. As Jake's lips laid claim to each nipple, Andy ran her fingers through his thick, wavy hair, tugging intermittently at the strands as his magical lips set her body quivering.

Breathing in his heady male aroma, the mixture of scents she knew so well, touching, probing, teasing every inch of his body that she loved so tenderly, Andy felt overwhelmed with passion, reaching even greater heights of mindless ecstasy than all the times before. In a fluid motion she ran her fingers down his broad chest, her palms sliding provocatively over his hardened nipples. When she lightly spun tantalizing circles from his hip bone to his thigh, he groaned with lusty pleasure. Her mouth followed the lines her fingers had traced, her darting tongue flickering with feverish movements down his body. And then slowly as she reached his calf, her mouth moved back up his virile form until she returned to his waiting, hungry lips. Before she allowed him possession, she nipped his lower lip seductively. When Jake finally claimed her mouth, their deeply passionate kiss filled them both with desperate, electrifying desire.

Her pulse raced wildly as Jake's muscled legs slid between hers, his hands intimately reaching under the curve below her buttocks to lift her up to meet his demanding thrusts.

Flying together to uncharted regions, their minds and bodies were enveloped in an ethereal mist. When at last they peaked, they both cried out in deep, primal abandon. Her rapturous release was so exquisite, Andy could taste salty tears of pleasure as they fell gently on her lips. Pressing her hands lovingly on either side of Jake's face, she felt a moistness at the edge of his eyes as well.

She adored the aftermath of lovemaking, the feel of Jake's relaxed body curving in to mold perfectly to hers. She loved the tender touch of his fingers leisurely stroking her forehead and gliding through her pleasure-dampened strands of hair. She loved the feel of his gentle lips lightly planting kisses in the crook of her neck. And most of all, she loved hearing him tell her how wonderful it was each time and how much he loved her.

Tonight as she nuzzled against the downy cloud of his chest hairs, listening to his heart return to a steady, even beat, Jake tenderly lifted her face to his. Kissing her softly on the tip of her nose, he said, "I've gone along with you all this time being a closet lover. But I have no intention, beautiful, of being a closet husband."

Her half-closed eyes flew open in shock. It was the first time Jake had ever mentioned marriage in any concrete terms. Her feelings suddenly began swirling around chaotically inside her head, her muscles tensing up. It had been safe to think about and even fantasize about marrying Jake, but now that he was presenting her with the reality, she felt overwhelmed, and more than a little scared.

She started to open her mouth trying to form some coherent words, but Jake gently yet firmly pressed her head back down on his chest. "Sleep on it," he said with lazy amusement.

CHAPTER NINE

The topic of marriage did not come up again for the next few weeks. Maybe Jake was giving himself, as well as Andy, some more time to digest the possibility. Andy was relieved to put the idea on the back burner for the time being. The whole work scene and its concomitant friction with Jake was distressing enough without further complications.

Andy again began thinking of her vow several months ago to scout around for other job possibilities. She had become so embroiled with Jake that she never did more than a superficial scanning of the job market. All the energy that she exerted in contending with her relationship with Jake had sapped a good deal of her drive and ambition.

A comment of Jake's flashed back into her mind. That day, months ago, on the running track, he had accused her of using work and getting ahead to hide from her feelings. She had been furious at his assumption then, but she was honest enough to admit there was some truth to his remark. Especially after her heartbreak over Ken, she began using work to escape all the pain and anger that relationship had produced. And it worked. The more energy she put into her job and the stronger she focused her attentions on stepping up the ladder at Horizons, the less time she spent thinking about Ken, and the better she slept at night. Even after she resolved her feelings about that dismal affair, she found that work had become a protection against other possible personal wounds.

In the process, Andy realized now, she had become deeply dependent on Horizons for her sustenance and nurturance. Having stepped into the company straight out of college, it was the only place of work Andy had ever known. And the idea of leaving felt very much like leaving home for the first time. It was terrifying. Horizons had become her family. Even the hassles and aggravations were part and parcel of home life. It was safe and comfortable. And even if she had to bide her time a little longer than she wanted, she would eventually move up the ladder.

At one moment she was filled with the conviction that it really was time to find a job with another company and free herself from her dependency on Horizons. The next moment she was furious with the notion, feeling like she was being forced to leave mainly because of Jake. She'd start to wish he had never left Chicago. Then she would have been safely entrenched in the sales coordinator position, happily planning for her next step up on the rise to fame and fortune. But of course then she never would have found Jake. And she loved him with every fiber of her being, regardless of the fact that he had complicated her life beyond her imagination.

Why the hell couldn't life be simple, she groaned to herself as she tossed her scheduling calendar back on her desk. She began twisting a loose strand of hair around her index finger, a nervous habit from childhood, and one she had overcome until recently.

The sound of her intercom made her let go of the strand guiltily.

"You've got a call on line 1 from Karen Peters."

"Thanks, Sheila."

"Oh, Andy, are those schedules ready for me to type?"

"Uhm—almost," Andy stammered, ashamed at herself for having been unable to concentrate on them all morning. Usually she had them in to Sheila for typing a day ahead of time. But lately a lot of her work was falling behind. She was going to have to shove her constant thoughts about her personal life into a little cubicle for a while and start paying more attention to her work. Pressing down the second button on her phone, she greeted Karen glumly.

"And a miserable morning to you too." Karen chuckled. "Don't you know you're always supposed to answer your work phone with cheery exuberance?"

"If I could find any cheery exuberance around, believe me, I would pay a lot for it."

"I thought things were going to start to look up once Jake got busy with Jim and MX Software."

Andy idly began to doodle on the corner of her message pad. "That is moving along. Jake has really been ecstatic about the project. Foster looked a little green at our last meeting with him about how much money it's costing. This is going to be one of the most expensive studies we've ever done. Of course, the old man's also sitting down in his office fantasizing about all the additional prestige this will bring Horizons, never mind all the extra moola."

"So why do you sound so bummed out?" Karen asked warmly.

"My mind feels like it has been caught in a whirlpool." Andy sighed, her swirling doodles mirroring her mood perfectly. "I can't figure out what to do about work, what to do about Jake, what to do about anything."

"Stop worrying. You'll come up with the answers. You always do."

"I may be carted away to the funny farm in the meantime." Andy laughed halfheartedly.

"Well, maybe a nice little rest in some exclusive nuthouse is just the thing for what ails you," Karen teased. "You could play badminton, volleyball, croquet, and come back a new woman."

"Watch it." Andy laughed. "The idea is beginning to sound appealing."

"Listen, Andy, why don't you just marry the guy, quit your job, and raise a team of little Downings?"

"You are simply filled with marvelous ideas this

morning, and that coming from one of the leading proponents of women's lib in Boston."

"Well, what's one woman's cup of tea could be another woman's poison." Karen chuckled.

"The tea still tastes too good to me. I'm afraid I'm addicted." Andy's tone switched to a more serious note. "I really can't figure out how Jake and I are going to sort all this out. I keep thinking my only option is to quit Horizons, but if I did, I might end up regretting my decision and in the process resenting Jake all the more. Sometimes I wish I wasn't so madly in love with him."

"Cheer up. I really do think it will all get sorted out. Don't they say love always finds a way?"

"So the saying goes." Andy smiled.

"Why don't we get together for dinner one night this week, and we'll map out the perfect plan?" Karen suggested.

"That sounds wonderful. How about tonight?"

"You really do want to get this issue resolved, don't you?" Karen laughed. "It's a date. Let's meet at Charley's at seven."

Andy felt more relaxed after saying good-bye to Karen, and she rapidly completed the scheduling calendar, dropping it off on Sheila's desk on her way down to show Jake some of her proposals for the MX account. Sheila called her back just as she stepped into the hall.

"Sally buzzed. She said Foster wants to see you on the double. Very important, Sally emphasized."

Andy shrugged. She couldn't imagine what could be that urgent, but she told Sheila she'd go right down. She decided to drop off the proposals with Jake now and speak with him about them after her powwow with Foster.

Jake's office was one flight below. Hurrying down the hall on his floor, she saw Jake bombing out of his office. He was walking toward her. Walking wasn't the right word. He stormed down the hall like the tornado straight out of *The Wizard of Oz*. Something was definitely wrong in the state of Kansas. He had that same look on his face she had seen the time he had barged in to her apartment when she had been with Daniel Reed—the one that looked like he was about to devour everything in his path. Andy waited for him to get to her. When he got near, she smiled tentatively, hoping to calm him down a little and learn what had gotten him so riled.

Jake swept by her, nearly knocking her into the wall in the process. She pivoted around, flabbergasted.

"Jake!" She practically had to shout, he had moved so quickly. Running after him, she called out for him to stop. He came to a sudden halt, spinning around to face her as she caught up with him.

"What in heaven's name is the matter?" she said irritably. No matter what he might be peeved about at work, he certainly had no business behaving that way toward her.

Jake glared at her with such intense rage that Andy physically stepped back. Her astonishment quickly made her anger evaporate. "Jake," she entreated, her voice now filled with concern. "What is it? What happened?"

"Well, babe, I've got to tip my hat to you. You really are something. And I thought you didn't know how to play dirty. Sweetheart, you could write the definitive book on the subject."

Never had Andy seen a more deadly smile or one filled with such cool hatred as the one Jake wore for her right then. But his voice was perfectly calm and in control. He finished his little speech by flicking an imaginary hat and swung around. Andy snatched his sleeve.

"What the hell are you talking about?" Andy's anger again surfaced. "You're obviously accusing me of some horrendous crime, and I can't even figure out what the charges are against me."

Jake easily shook free of Andy's grasp. He took a step toward her, and for one awful moment she thought he was going to hit her. Her hands trembled, her heart pounding so loudly against her chest she thought it might erupt. But she stood her ground, staring into his dark eyes. "Jake . . ." His name fell off her lips more as a cry than a word.

Without another sound he turned from her and walked away. Andy watched him disappear down the stairs. Teeth clenched, she fought for breath. It finally clicked that Foster's urgent order to meet with her might well shed some light on this insane business. Calling on every muscle in her body to function, she made her way down to Foster's office.

Sally looked very relieved to see her.

"Oh, good." Sally sighed. "Foster's had me buzz your office two more times. He just took a phone call, but he wants to talk with you posthaste."

"What's going on?" Andy asked, trying to regulate her breathing.

"You haven't seen this morning's paper?"

As Andy shook her head, Sally turned the front page of the business section across the desk.

Andy's eyes scanned the sheet. With a gasp she spotted in the upper right hand column the heading, "Data Base Sues MX Software." Quickly reading, she discovered that James Hart was being brought up on charges of company espionage. While employed as a systems analyst at Data Base, he allegedly stole plans for a series of new software products that were to be brought out in the fall. Not only was MX expected to file immediate bankruptcy proceedings, James Hart would very likely face criminal charges.

Holding the paper in her hands, Andy gaped at Sally.

"I can't believe it." Her shock momentarily pushed her encounter with Jake from her mind. Then slowly she began to make the connection.

"Oh, God, Foster must have been livid when he saw this. He's out a fortune to say nothing of the bruise to the company's reputation."

"Well"—Sally dropped her voice down low, quickly checking the lit button on her phone to make sure Foster was still on the line—"that's not all he's out. He and Jake just had a knockdown verbal brawl in there."

"Foster fired him?" Andy asked, astonished.

"I wasn't eavesdropping, believe me," Sally confided. "But the two of them were loud enough to be heard clear down the block. I don't really know if Mr. Foster would have fired Jake, although I've never heard him get so riled. He called Jake an impulsive hothead, claiming he should have checked MX out more thoroughly before getting so involved. After Jake got finished ranting back, he told Foster he was quitting, and he barged out of here looking like he was about to commit murder."

Andy nodded silently, thinking to herself, he did commit murder. He just up and killed our relationship. Exactly why his fury transferred from Foster to her wasn't yet clear to her. But that he somehow held her responsible, believing she had pulled some underhanded stunt, was obvious.

A few more pieces of the puzzle fit after her terse meeting with Foster. Without any preamble, he told her to get things in order in her department by the end of the week, at which time she would become Horizons' new sales coordinator, Larry Butson taking over her old position. He never even asked her if she still wanted it. And Andy was too speechless to sift it all through anyway.

She sat in her office mulling it over and over again in her mind. Jake believed Andy had set him up intentionally with MX. But why would he think she would want to discredit him? Surely not to get his job—not that way. What would ever make him believe she would do such a lousy thing? And he talked about trust. Damn him, she muttered fiercely, slamming the top drawer of her desk so hard papers flew all over the floor.

The final piece of the puzzle came later that afternoon. Larry rapped lightly on her door, and then walked in, not waiting for a response.

"I need to talk to you about something," he said softly.

"Not now, please Larry." Andy quickly picked up the first paper her hand lit on. "I've—I've got too much to do."

Larry paid no attention and sat down across from her, his hands resting lightly on her desk.

"It's about Jake."

Andy's eyes shot up. "What is it?"

"I don't relish the role of squealer, but I owe you a hell of a lot more than I owe Sandra Kennedy."

Andy sat up straighter in her seat, her eyes glued to Larry. "What does Sandra have to do with Jake?"

"My devious little co-worker must have read today's paper, and it seems she paid Jake a visit this morning, informing him that you and your friend Karen Peters intentionally set him up. She told him she heard you and Karen gloating over the phone at his having gotten involved with a company that Karen already knew was under investigation."

"But that's crazy," Andy gasped, completely stunned by Larry's news. "Why, Karen was even thinking of investing some of her own money in MX. For all I know, she might already have done it."

"Sandra can be very persuasive, I'm afraid. From what I overheard her telling Diane, Jake bought the story verbatim. Especially after Sandra told him you had spouted off to her as well as other staff members about your determination to push him out of the company and get his job."

"She purposely distorted everything I said. Sure, when Jake first came here, I let off some steam on occasion. I may have even said he'd never make it at Horizons. But I never gave one person in this place a single reason to believe I would do anything personally to get rid of him."

"I know," Larry assured her. "I work here too, remember?"

Andy flushed. "Of course. I'm sorry. I'm just so . . ." She stopped short. Everything was such a mess, she wasn't sure what she was feeling. She sat back in her chair, staring at Larry, a dazed expression on her face.

"Did I really get up this morning, or is this some horrendous nightmare that my alarm clock is going to rescue me from?" She gave Larry a mournful look.

"It's a nightmare, all right. But not the kind you sleep through, unfortunately. Why don't you talk with Jake and try to straighten it out?"

Andy sat quietly. Then in a voice blended with anger and pain, she said, "I don't know. I have to think about it. I have to think about it very carefully."

After Larry slipped around the desk to give her a supportive hug, he left her alone. It was well after five o'clock, but she made no move to leave. She felt split in half as she sat at her desk trying to make sense out of her feelings. One side of her wanted to race over to Jake's apartment, explain the whole thing, and try to resolve the dreadful misunderstanding. But the other half felt painfully betrayed. Jake had said he loved her, even talked about marriage, and yet he bought Sandra's story without question. And he was the one always preaching about trust.

Finally, she started off for home, not having resolved what to do. As she stepped into her apartment house, Jake was locking his door. A large suitcase rested next to him on the floor. Lifting it up again, he saw her standing there.

"Where are you going?" Andy asked, immediately angry at herself for showing any interest.

"Don't get your hopes up that I'm skipping out of town. I have no intention of easing your conscience. Just taking a brief vacation. I need some clean, fresh air to cleanse me. But you can count on my return. Horizons is most definitely not the only fish in the sea. I'll be around, sweetheart. You can count on it. And you can be damn sure the next place I go will not be headed by some antiquarian who hasn't had a creative thought in his head for the last thirty years." Starting for the door, he stopped abruptly. Looking back over his shoulder, he said coolly, "Actually, you fit in perfectly. You finally have what you wanted all along. Good luck." The words sounded decidedly more like "drop dead."

Andy hadn't said another word. Her only consolation was that he had resolved for her any ambivalence she had felt about the way to handle this whole thing. Hell could freeze over before she would ever stoop to explaining the truth to Jake. And this time there was no amusement in her use of the old catchall saying. She meant it.

The phone was ringing when she opened the door

to her apartment. Her feet felt like lead as she walked over to answer it.

"Hey, what the hell are you doing there?" Karen's irritated voice snapped.

"Huh?"

"Andy, I have been sitting at the bar at Charley's for the past twenty minutes. If you don't get down here pronto, I'm going to run off with one of the dozens of men who have already propositioned me."

She had totally forgotten about her date for dinner with Karen. It felt like a lifetime had gone by since she'd talked to her that morning.

Wearily she said, "I'm sorry, Karen. Something's come up. I—I can't talk about it right now. Could we make it another night? The thought of eating is enough to make me sick."

"I'll come over. Be there in fifteen minutes." Karen hung up before Andy could refuse her offer.

Karen was dumbfounded when Andy showed her the morning paper. Her copy had been innocently waiting at her front door since dawn. Having gotten up late this morning, she hadn't bothered with it until now.

"I can't believe it. Jim seemed so straightforward and honest. I was really beginning to think this guy was something special." Karen stared at the newspaper as she spoke.

"I'm sorry, Karen. I've been so caught up with how this whole thing has affected me that I didn't give enough thought to how devastated you would feel by this whole disaster." Andy put Karen's cup

161

of coffee on the wicker basket and sat down beside her.

"Did he get any money out of you?" Andy asked gently.

"Money? No—not money, just a piece of my heart. Albeit a small piece, but still every piece counts." Karen looked into Andy's concerned face. "It isn't nearly as awful as losing your whole heart. I'd like to give Jake Downing a piece of my mind."

Andy frowned. "Oh, no. I don't want you to say a word to him. Anyway"—she smiled—"you've got to stop giving pieces of yourself away. First your heart, now your mind. No. I believe there's a lesson in all of this. At least for me. And that's to start holding on to all my pieces." Tears spiked her eyes. "I just wish I knew how to put myself together again. Now I know how Humpty-Dumpty felt."

She'd been running too hard. She knew it, and yet it had become impossible to slow down. Running herself ragged seemed the only way she could keep herself together. Clocking twelve miles a day or more was not the way to prepare for the marathon. By the time April came around, she'd be too exhausted to race. But some unknown force drove her to push herself to the limit each time she ran. She was scared —scared that if she stopped she would fall apart.

Jake had been back in town for a month. A couple of weeks ago he signed on with King and Langner as their head sales coordinator. No doubt, she decided when she heard the news at work, they felt that they would do best having Jake on their team rather than

162

risking him going off somewhere else and continuing to steal accounts from them. So now, once again, she and Jake were rivals. Jake had not yet invaded her territory, but she knew it was just a matter of time.

They hardly ever bumped into each other at the apartment house, but when they did, they behaved like barely polite strangers. Andy could count on one hand the number of words they'd spoken. It was fine with her. They no longer had anything to say to each other.

As she continued her practice run up the section of the marathon course known as Heartbreak Hill, she began to feel a pull in her side. Heartbreak Hill was aptly named. The last long run of the marathon, it was all uphill and painfully taxing even to the best runners. Andy was feeling far from the best. She had quit Nautilus after her breakup with Jake, and her home routine had lacked spirit and zeal. All the fight seemed knocked out of her. It was only the running itself that offered her heart and mind any relief from her tortured thoughts.

The ache in her side suddenly threatened to floor her. Added to the pain, the dark, bleakly cold March morning bit through her Windbreaker past her thermal layers to her skin. Grabbing hold of her waist, she slowed down, breathing heavily as she leaned against a large oak tree on the grassy median strip. As she took a deep breath, she buckled slightly as a stabbing pain shot through her chest.

Forcing herself to relax her muscles and take small, steady breaths, the pain in her side and chest began to subside. Resting against the tree, she saw

163

another runner coming up the road. He ran easily, showing little sign of exertion. Andy found herself envying his relaxed, unhurried stride. As he drew nearer, her breath caught, the slow, steady rhythm of her heart going immediately to hell.

Jake recognized her at the same moment. She was certain he would continue past her, and she struggled to keep her eyes averted. Her sudden shivering as he ran toward her had nothing to do with the cold.

"Are you all right?" Jake's question was posed with a tone of casual concern as he stopped in front of her.

She could have told him the truth; that she hadn't been all right since he stormed out of her life, not by a long shot; but she strove for the same cool manner in her voice. "I'm fine."

"It's kind of cold to stay still for too long."

Her mind willed him to go, but he continued to stand there, gazing at her. His look became even more intent, brows furrowed, the tiny scar on his mouth lost in his tight-lipped grimace.

"Tell me something, Andy. Was it worth it? Is the job everything you hoped for, everything you fought for?" Once the questions started, more spurted out. "Did you and Karen think it would somehow be a perfect plan? Did you think I would never discover the truth behind it? Did you think I'd happily go skipping off to another job and then all your problems would be solved? Did you intend for us to still get married once I was finally out of Horizons—a marriage based on an insidious lie?" He threw the

164

questions at her in a rage that became more fierce with each one.

Andy's hands cuffed her ears, wanting to drown out his attack.

"Stop it, damn you! Stop it," she finally screamed, the tears streaming unbidden down her cheeks. "It's all lies, hateful lies. Sandra handed you a gift-wrapped box of lies, and you grabbed it, thanking her for her present. Oh, she really wanted to get back at me, but I never thought she would stoop that low. And what's worse, far worse, is that I never imagined you would believe me capable of something so base and underhanded."

"Don't try dragging Sandra down now," he said sharply. "She told me how you had been harassing her for months. Every time she came up with an innovative approach to a protocol, you were so threatened you refused to acknowledge its value. You would have had her fired only you both knew her work was too good, and you didn't have a leg to stand on. You'd been pushing her so hard, checking every single thing she did, that the poor kid was almost at the breaking point when she came to me. She didn't even want to tell me what had happened; I had to practically force it out of her." His eyes burned down into hers.

"She's a remarkable girl. I'll hand her that. And very diligent where you are concerned. Although maybe she didn't even have to bother trying so hard. You probably would have bought her story without all the extra work she put into it." Andy spoke calmly, though she was chilled to the bone and utterly

165

devastated. She had used her trump card. Telling Jake the truth had been her final toss. But he didn't show the slightest inclination to believe her.

It was over—finally and irrevocably over. An icy numbness set in, and with a sad, hollow laugh, she said, "And once upon a time you were going to teach me about the virtue of trust."

The worst part of it all was that she still wanted him, her body still craved his touch beyond all reason. The loving within her that Jake had awakened and nurtured all those months was hard put to die. Shoving her frozen hands into her pockets, Andy left Jake standing there and ran the rest of Heartbreak Hill.

CHAPTER TEN

He was standing on the edge of the pier, sandy hair tousled by the winds, shirt sleeves rolled up revealing strong, muscled forearms. Back to the sea, he gazed across the long wooden wharf to her, dark eyes lovingly beckoning her to come to him, arms open and inviting.

Andy started to walk tentatively toward Jake, uncertain whether he truly meant for her to come. As she drew closer and saw the gentle, tender smile softening his rugged features, his lips mouthing her name with longing, she began to run to him. He was further away than he appeared, and somehow the faster she ran the longer the pier stretched out to the sea. Her eyes stared yearningly into his as she began to race more swiftly to his outstretched arms. Soon she was flying, her feet barely touching the wooden slats—soaring to her beloved. At last she was almost at his side. She reached out to clasp his hand, and in that instant he vanished.

A vast, dark sea stretched out before her. Inexorably she raced toward the edge of the pier unable to stop, knowing all the while she was heading for utter oblivion. And as her feet left the last board and she began to tumble into the awesome void beyond, she began to scream.

Bolting upright in bed, Andy fought for breath. She was drenched with perspiration, body trembling, chest heaving. A nightmare, she laughed shakily, comforting herself; only a nightmare.

It was not the first. The places were never the same, but Jake was always there, calling out to her, opening his arms to embrace her. Andy always would start racing to him, only to see him disappear, yet she was never able to stop, inevitably plummeting to some terrible, unavoidable doom.

Andy reached over to her end table for a tissue to wipe her brow. Her alarm clock read four A.M. Too early to get up. Besides, if she didn't get some rest, the exhaustion at work would be unbearable.

Exhaustion had become her general state of being. Not only her rigid, strenuous running schedule but her intense absorption with her new job sapped every ounce of her strength. She had lost over five pounds, which on her already slender frame could not be spared. She was bone-weary, but she kept driving herself. Maybe it wasn't the healthiest approach, but it did effectively keep Jake out of her mind during her waking hours. Now if she could only find some way to keep him out of her dreams.

She was still in love with him. No matter how much she fueled her rage with remembrances of the pain he had inflicted on her by his ugly distrust, it didn't manage to touch the core of her being. Her love still held reign there, beyond all reason. She kept telling herself that her yearning and desire for him would lessen in time, but days had rolled into weeks and nothing had changed.

Andy could fill all her empty, lonely waking hours with running and working, but there were always those minutes before sleep overtook her when she lay alone in the large bed with only memories of Jake's loving embrace enveloping her. Over and over her mind would roam his long, muscled body, remembering every curve, every sensitive loving spot she had caressed and marked as her own. It was insane to allow herself to think that way, serving no purpose other than to increase the pain that was already only barely tolerable.

Yawning, she sank back down on her pillows, tugging the down comforter up to her chin. Forcing her eyes to shut and willing her body to relax, she finally began to feel herself drifting off. Within a few minutes her breathing deepened and evened as she fell back asleep.

Jake was standing on a balcony, high above the city, leaning against the low railing. His arms stretched out to her, and Andy began running toward him. . . .

The next morning, entering her office a few minutes late, Andy looked with curiosity at the large parcel resting on the floor in her outer office.

"What's in the box?" Andy inquired, slipping off her jacket and slinging it over the coatrack.

She could feel Sheila's eyes surveying her even before she turned around. At moments like this Andy almost regretted having brought her secretary along with her to her new department. Sheila had become a regular mother hen. Andy knew it was out of genuine concern, but it was not always easy to be confronted by Sheila's running commentary on her slow disintegration. Suddenly wishing that she had applied a little more makeup to camouflage the dark circles under her eyes, Andy kept her head slightly averted as she walked over to the desk to gather her mail.

Disregarding Andy's question about the package, Sheila handed her the pile of pink message slips.

"You look lousy." Sheila's harsh observation was tempered by the warm concern reflected in her big blue eyes.

"Thanks," Andy replied wryly, looking directly at her secretary. No point in trying to avert her gaze. Sheila had the eyes of an eagle and a mouth the size of Niagara. "Somehow I guessed you would have something nice to say to me this morning." Andy slipped an errant lock of hair behind her ear. She had been so wiped out this morning from her restless night that she had overslept, missing her regular morning run, and not even sparing the time to pull her hair back in a neat chignon.

"Let me tell you something my mother always said when things looked bleak." Sheila spoke with philosophic calm.

"Oh, Sheila, I beg you, spare me one of your mother's syllogisms this morning," Andy entreated with a grin.

"You need a little pick-me-up," Sheila insisted, a determined finger pointing at her.

"If you dare to tell me your mother said, 'it's always darkest before the dawn,' I will personally strangle you and then go after your mom." Andy glared at Sheila with mock menace.

"Mother is not that trite," Sheila retorted. "What Mother wisely told me in my darkest moments was 'Sheila, sweetheart, no man's worth it!'"

They both broke out into hysterical laughter.

"Oh, Sheila, sweetheart, tell me, what would I do without you?" Andy grinned affectionately.

"You'd probably go off into blissful decay." Sheila chuckled, and then sobering, she added, "But as long as I'm watching over you, I don't intend to sit back and let you go down the tubes. If you don't start adding a little flesh to those jutting bones, I'm going to start force-feeding you some of Mother's chicken soup."

"I'll eat, I'll eat," Andy promised, moving over to the large box.

"What is this thing, anyway?" Andy stooped down to examine the carton.

"UPS brought it in this morning. It's addressed to you. I hope for your sake it's a five-year supply of vitamins and pep pills."

Andy looked over her shoulder and stuck her tongue out at her secretary. "Toss me the letter opener. Let's see what's inside."

Opening the last flap of the box, Andy sat down on the floor, laughing. "Look." She chuckled, pulling out one of at least two dozen large cans stacked inside. "It's a five-year supply, all right—but not of vitamins." She read the label out loud to Sheila. " 'Colonel Winston's Grits,' the Southern answer to the dull Boston baked bean.' So the good colonel is going to do it after all."

"But the marketing report we sent him didn't exactly reflect any avid desire for a gritty answer to the bean." Sheila laughed, walking over to examine the can.

"Some people believe in taking risks even when there are no signs at all pointing to success." She paused, reflecting over her comment. "I can't decide if I admire people like that or think they're utter fools."

Straightening up, Andy smoothed out her skirt. Pulling back her shoulders, she walked quietly into her office. Sheila didn't say another word.

Andy leaned back in her chair and closed her eyes. Normally, her morning run energized her for the day ahead. Without it she felt it hard to face the ever-mounting pile of work on her desk.

For the hundredth time since becoming sales coordinator, Andy wondered whether she should have taken it on. She remembered wanting the position so badly, thinking it was somehow going to make a major difference in her life. Now it seemed mainly to give her more stress, more work, and more problems. What it didn't give her was satisfaction.

The job wasn't the problem. Her attitude had been

172

the thing that had changed. Even when she was at the peak of concentration, willing every inch of her mind to focus on the demanding work, it did not provide the fulfillment she had expected. Would it have been any different, she pondered, if Jake hadn't been here first?

There he was again. Just barely offscreen waiting for the slightest opening to leap out in Vistavision Technicolor. Some self-destructive force inside her head persisted in dragging him back on the screen each time. Her most frequent vision was of him running along the track, his body glistening, every muscle clearly defined as he raced with those self-assured, long, easy strides.

The Boston Marathon was less than a week away. When they had been together, Jake sometimes teased Andy about having a justice of the peace waiting at the finish line. Did he ever think about those joking times, those happy times when their love seemed to override all obstacles? Then, she had felt as though she could fly down those twenty-six miles on wings of ecstasy. Thinking about the marathon now, the miles seemed endless. She was worried, admitting to herself that she had chronically overtrained, in the process becoming stale. The race still meant a great deal to her, although the reasons had changed. It had become more than a love of the sport and the accomplishment of a difficult feat. It even went beyond a challenge of endurance, a test of strength and will. Andy had gotten it into her head that running the marathon would somehow exorcise Jake from her heart. Rational thought did not deter her from her belief.

She compelled herself to open her eyes and face the morass on the top of her desk, promising herself a nice, long run after work. Later that evening she and Karen would be getting together with a few other friends to go over the game plan for the marathon, picking the various locations to set up water stations along the route. Karen had already begun organizing and orchestrating the whole thing. Andy was unendingly grateful, not only for the help, but for the desperately needed boost to her morale.

Tackling the nearly completed proposal on the top of her "In" basket, Andy was relieved about one thing. Jake had continued to stay clear of her clients, even most of her prospective ones. She wondered if, knowing Horizons territory, he was making it a point to expand and create other regions. It would have been easy to learn more about what he was doing. Andy knew a couple of people at King and Langner well enough to check Jake's territory out, but she had intentionally not pursued her contacts. The less she knew about Jake's life the better.

They still ran into each other on a few occasions, mostly at home, but a couple of times at Friday's, a local café that was always filled with an after-work business crowd. Their pattern of impersonal civility continued. Once or twice Andy thought Jake seemed a fraction less rigid, sensing a minuscule softening of his features when he said a perfunctory hello, but then she would convince herself it was a delusion born of her own weakness for hoping against hope.

Then the compulsory anger set in. Why was she looking for his forgiveness anyway? She was the injured party, not him.

Over the more than six weeks since they had parted, Andy had found her anger harder to sustain. Not that she still didn't believe Jake was at fault, but being justified did not seem to balance against the weightier emptiness and loss. Sometimes it all seemed so meaningless. The triteness began to get to her more and more, her anger starting to run a far second.

The lounge at Friday's was bustling with the large crowd of hangers-on from "happy hour." A sea of men uniformed by Brooks Brothers and a large sprinkling of women in their Filene's business outfits crowded around the long oak bar. Friday's was the "in place" in the Back Bay. It had all the accoutrements of this year's kitsch: Tiffany lamps, streetside greenhouse, daguerreotypes of Boston lining the walls, soft rock on the best Bose speakers, and its true appeal, king-size drinks.

Andy made her way to Karen's table. Invariably, after too much time at this place, Andy would get a headache, caused by a combination of all the hubbub and the acrid smoke that filled the congested space. Tonight, having once again run a longer distance than she'd vowed she would, the pounding in her head attacked her almost as soon as she had stepped in the door.

When she and Jake had been together, both being nonsmokers and lovers of peace and quiet, they had

175

resolutely avoided coming here. Andy was especially religious about not showing up at Friday's with Jake because three quarters of Horizons seemed to always stop by there for after-work relaxation.

Lately she had forced herself to join the group from work on occasion. It was self-prescribed medicine and it worked, except for the few times she bumped into Jake there with a group from King and Langner. After those encounters, the rest of her evening was always shot.

Tonight she quickly scanned the place to make sure Jake wasn't there. Satisfied, she joined Karen and the others.

Laughing over drinks about some of the more humorous pitfalls of marathon racing, like breaking a bra strap or splitting your shorts, Andy found herself relaxing and getting into the spirit of the marathon. After a couple of hours, the whole group seemed happy about the plan, everyone knowing where they would be manning a water station and where they'd meet to cheer Andy on at the finish. Jane Robinson, one of Andy's college friends, promised to keep a supply of safety pins on her—just in case.

Saying a warm good night to her friends, Andy and Karen lingered a little longer over their half-finished piña coladas.

"Do you know that's the first genuine smile I've seen on your face in almost two months?"

"Please, Karen, don't you start on me now. Sheila's enough mother hen for any person." Andy gave her friend a woeful grimace.

"I won't cluck." Karen smiled. "But I am concerned about you. Are you sure you're going to manage the marathon? We both know how drained you are—physically and emotionally."

"Karen, I'm going to be fine. Honest."

In a soft voice, Karen said, "I ran into Jake last weekend at a party."

Andy shot Karen a tense glance. "Was he alone?"

"Alone and looking equally as miserable as you." Karen sighed.

"Well, I guess that's some consolation. Oddly, it doesn't make me feel any better."

"I really wish the two of you hadn't gotten so damn messed up," Karen cursed, her brows furrowing.

"Let's not start on my most depressing topic of conversation." Andy's green eyes narrowed.

"I just hope if you see him at the marathon you won't get thrown."

"Jake has already thrown me as much as is humanly possible. Anyway, there are going to be more than seven thousand racers lining up on Monday morning. In that whole sea of bodies I doubt Jake is going to stand out."

What she told Karen wasn't true. Jake would always stand out a mile, no matter how big the crowd. In spite of it all, he was still one in a million.

Andy was just in front of Karen as they stepped outside of Friday's. Jake was approaching the door from the street at the same time. They both stopped, their eyes immediately connecting. Then showing no hesitation, Jake walked up to her.

"I need to talk with you," he said without preamble.

Andy's voice stuck in her throat, and all she could do was shake her head from side to side.

"Please—one drink. Don't say no."

Karen stepped up to Andy. "I have to get home. Go ahead, have another drink. You could use it."

Before Andy had a chance to balk, Karen rushed off, and Jake swung her by the elbow back into the café. They found a tiny table in the back of the bar.

"I don't want a drink," Andy said firmly. "Tell me what you want to say." Her harsh tone belied the utter havoc she felt inside. She clasped her hands tightly on the table to keep them from trembling.

"I've been doing a lot of thinking—about why I was so quick to believe you had betrayed me." He looked across at her, his features tense. "I could give you a dozen rationalizations and stack my case with a lot of circumstantial evidence, but I guess the real truth is . . ." He paused, taking a deep breath. "I was scared. I warned you I was a runner. I think when I realized the depth of our commitment, it also made me see the potential power that it gave you to hurt me—to destroy me. I'm not proud to admit it, but the thought terrified me, so I ran. I didn't even realize what I was actually feeling."

Andy sat stoically quiet while he spoke. His words were honest and touching, but they were coming long after she had needed to hear them.

"Well"—she sighed wearily—"you can stop being afraid. It's over."

"I'm not afraid any longer. I realize the risk of

178

getting hurt is nothing compared to the pain of being without you." He looked imploringly at her, but Andy's face offered no forgiveness.

"It's too late. I needed you, Jake, when I was down and hurting, but you weren't there. And I can't trust that you ever will be."

"You're wrong." He caught hold of her hand as she rose. She tugged it free.

"Maybe. And maybe I don't want to take any more risks of getting hurt myself." When she walked away from his table, Jake silently watched her leave.

The sleepy little town of Hopkinton, Massachusetts had found its place of fame in the annals of running history as the starting point of the Boston Marathon since 1924. Throngs of people, a veritable sea of bodies, gathered together on this cool, fifty-five-degree Monday morning. Intentionally coinciding with the state holiday, Patriots' Day, the mass of spectators easily matched the numbers of racers.

Andy adjusted her number 5649 on the front of her tank top. Far from being a top ranker, she still felt an exhilarating high just having qualified for this prestigious event. The air was filled with tense expectancy, everyone trying to find any spot at all to do some final warm-up stretches.

Feeling foolish, Andy skirted her eyes around the monumental crowd of runners, trying to find Jake's face among them. There were a fair number of tall, sinewy-looking runners with sandy blond hair milling about, but none of them was Jake. She felt a sudden lurch of anxiety that he might not be here.

But of course he would. This race was as important to him as it was to her.

Andy tried to concentrate on her relaxation and breathing and not on the long, excruciating stretch ahead of her. Her mind, not cooperating, ran through the twenty-six-mile race, 26.2 miles to be exact, all the way to the Pru. The first big hill would be eighteen miles into the course on the road from Wellesley to Newton. That was the easy one. It was the second, backbreaking distance from Newton to Brookline, infamously but justifiably named Heart-break Hill, that was the real tough one. Andy had done enough practice runs on that hill to know just how tough. She prayed that when she made it through today she would not think about her devastating last encounter there with Jake.

Finally, Andy's group started off. That first kickoff was filled with all the excitement and elation that Andy had always fantasized. All of her worries about not being in perfect condition evaporated. She felt mentally tough, her concentration focusing on long, easy strides. It was of crucial importance to set a steady, even pace, being careful not to blow all one's energy in the first ten or fifteen miles only to come to the hardest stretch with nothing left to give.

She was feeling good, easily overriding the first pangs of tiredness and the initial pain and discomfort. She also knew there was plenty more ahead. Keeping in sync with a large group of other runners, Andy watched the spread slowly thin as they made their way through Ashland to Framingham. For the most part Andy was oblivious to the goings-on at the

180

periphery—the mass of spectators, the markers, the water stations.

Andy spotted Karen's wave at the borderline of Framingham, and without slowing down, she stretched out her hand for a paper cup of water. She didn't really need it, taking it more to give her friend the feeling that she was a part of the event. Giving Karen a thumbs-up sign as she passed, she heard her cheering loudly.

Further into Framingham another friend, Terry Bernard, waited for her at a second water station. Larry Butson and a couple of her other pals from Horizons also gathered there. In a sweat now, and feeling the more painful aches and tiredness, Andy found that second drink far more important than the first.

She was a little over twelve miles into the race. Pulse pounding, legs throbbing, chest tightening up, Andy's early confidence began to wane. She had been watching the mileage markers for the past few miles. It was a bad sign. When she was running at top form, she paced herself from within, not from taking note of the distance she had already covered and still had to face.

This first hill was not the breeze she had imagined. Her lack of balanced training really began to tell at this point. She found herself frequently out of sync, the pain especially bad in her hamstrings, which were beginning to tighten. She began looking in earnest for the next water station.

Karen had raced by car from Framingham to the Wellesley-Newton border and was waiting for Andy

181

as she came by. Karen looked with a worried frown at her friend. This time Andy slowed down to a snail's pace to get her cup of water and a slice of orange.

"Andy, you look awful. This isn't worth killing yourself over."

"I'm fine, I'm fine," she gasped breathlessly between gulps. Tossing the cup aside, she picked up speed.

By the start of Newton, two hours and fifteen minutes having gone by, Larry shouted out the news that Alberto Salazar had just won, breaking all past records. The news only added to Andy's mounting despair. No longer even thinking about setting a time goal for herself, she began to panic about the possibility of not finishing. She had to finish, she kept drilling herself, even if she fell dying over the finish line.

A large crowd of friends cheered her on with raucous screams and shouts as she started up Commonwealth Avenue. Buoyed by their exuberant, energetic spirit and cries of confidence, she began to get a second wind. She even spotted Ted Foster among the crowd, as boisterous and enthusiastic as the rest. Andy smiled. She decided she was going to make it after all.

At the very moment her confidence and determination reached its peak, she suddenly fell crashing to the ground. Stunned, Andy twisted her head around to see what had floored her. A pothole, not very deep, but enough to have caught her toe, was the diabolical culprit.

Runners continued on, veering around her, a couple of them shouting for her to get over to the median strip. Instead, Andy steadied her breath and got up carefully.

Damn it. A sharp pain stung her ankle. It was the same foot she had injured the year before in a preliminary race. It hurt painfully, but she was so furious at the stupidity of what had happened, it allowed her to endure the ache and slowly continue on.

Karen had spotted her fall, and she raced down the median, anxiously pushing through the thick mass of spectators, catching up with Andy as she started hobbling slightly back up Commonwealth Avenue.

"Andy, are you okay? You're limping!" Karen shouted at the top of her voice.

"No kidding," Andy shouted back, a determined glint in her eye. She was mad as hell, and it was pushing her forward relentlessly.

Almost like my dream, she thought with a sudden morbid flash. Running inexorably to doom. She had to keep reminding herself over and over that the end held victory not disaster.

Each step was becoming more painful now. She was almost at the end of Heartbreak Hill with still over three miles through Brookline to the finish line at the Pru. Tears kept slipping down her cheek. She was sweating profusely despite the relatively cool temperature, and every muscle, never mind her injured ankle, cried out at the injustice she was doing to her body. . . .

Less than a mile, she kept telling herself. Only the

183

stragglers ran with her now. Her cheering section had spread themselves out along the last half mile. Realizing her steadfast determination to see this through to the bitter end, they no longer entreated her to give it up. Shouting words of encouragement, they helped immeasurably to keep her going.

She was having difficulty focusing her vision. Between the fatigue, the sweat, and the wisps of hair that had escaped her ponytail, Andy could barely decipher where she was going. It was then that the final calamity struck. Swaying slightly, another runner, equally debilitated, ran in front of Andy, accidentally tripping her in the process. Screaming in pain, Andy crumpled to the ground.

Sobbing, more from the utter frustration than the pain, she knew with absolute certainty that there was no way she could get up again and continue. Less than one mile and she'd have made it. Crawling over to the curb, near fainting, nauseous, and aching from head to toe, Andy sank her head into her lap.

Karen saw the whole thing from halfway down the block and started toward Andy. She was crying too. Larry Butson caught hold of her arm, pointing straight ahead of him. Karen stopped, watching, the tears streaming down her cheeks.

Andy felt the weight of a large hand at the pit of her back. She didn't even have the strength to look up. Someone was kneeling beside her. Then two hands were on her shoulders, gently massaging the muscles.

There were no other hands in the world with that magic touch. Andy lifted her head and turned to see

Jake smiling at her. His hands continued their wondrous, hypnotic movements, tears and sweat shining on his face.

That smile. It was the one he wore in all those dreams. But this time it was real, and there was no fear inside of her that he would vanish.

"Put your arm around me," he whispered huskily.

She followed his gentle command. Carefully he helped her up, slipping his arm firmly around her waist. Andy shivered as she leaned heavily against him. It had been such a long time. His body never felt more wonderful.

Andy looked wearily down the long stretch of road. "I—I can hardly see the end in sight. I don't know if I can make it, Jake."

He encircled her in his arms, kissing her tear-stained cheeks, her eyes, and at last her lips. Hungrily they clung to each other.

"That's not the end down there, darling. It's the beginning. And we're going to make it there together. I may have had to travel a long road when it comes to trust, but with you beside me this road will be a cinch." He kissed her lips once more, the tenderness sweet beyond compare.

"I love you, Jake."

"Come on, beautiful, we have our race to win." Jake kissed her lightly on the cheek.

"I think we've already won," she whispered back. And then with a laugh she said, "But let's not disappoint our public." Karen and the rest of the crowd stood gathered together on the sidelines. There wasn't a dry eye in the group.

Catching hold of Andy's hand that was slung around his shoulder, and half lifting her with his other hand around her waist, they ran together to the finish line, knowing at last that only joy and happiness lay ahead.

LOOK FOR NEXT MONTH'S
CANDLELIGHT ECSTASY ROMANCES ®

Candlelight
Ecstasy Romances™

$1.95 each

MARIANNE HARVEY

Know the passions and perils, the love and the lust, as the best of the past is reborn in her books.

☐ STORMSWEPT	19030-4-13	$3.50
☐ THE DARK HORSEMAN	11758-5-44	3.50
☐ THE PROUD HUNTER	17098-2-32	3.50
☐ THE WILD ONE	19207-2-02	2.95

Writing as Mary Williams

☐ GYPSY FIRES	12860-9-13	2.95
☐ GYPSY LEGACY	12990-7-16	2.95

The primitive new world of these lovers was like their passion— savage and untamed.

This first book in the *New Zealander* series sweeps through exotic New Zealand with a tale of adventure and passion. It is the story of William Pollard, a deserter from a British warship, and Tairata, a beautiful Maori princess. Together they embark on a perilous journey through a primitive land. 11125-0-99 $3.95

THE CASTAWAY

Aaron Fletcher